Vine:
An Urban
Legend

Vine: An Urban Legend

Michael Williams

SEVENTH STAR PRESS

Cover art and design: Enggar Adirasa

Cover art in this book copyright © 2018 Enggar Adirasa & Seventh Star Press, LLC.

Editor: Karen M. Leet

Published by Seventh Star Press, LLC.

ISBN Number: 978-1-948042-62-8

Seventh Star Press

www.seventhstarpress.com

info@seventhstarpress.com

Publisher's Note:

Vine: An Urban Legend is a work of fiction. All names, characters, and places are the product of the author's imagination, used in fictitious manner. Any resemblances to actual persons, places, locales, events, etc. are purely coincidental.

Printed in the United States of America

Second Edition

For Mark Blum

Author's Note:

Vine is a wedding of Greek tragedy and urban legend. It is a choral novel, a story told by a number of voices. Episodes recount the narrative action, while choruses of various kinds—Prologue, Parodos, Stasima, and Exodos—comment and reflect on what is happening. Each section's title sets forth its purpose, and each chorus section designates who speaks it.

1 Prologue: Tommy

(Enter T. TOMMY BRISCOE, dressed in a gold lamé jumpsuit, caped and pompadoured. Behind him enter the BRISCHORDS: a man and woman dressed in biker leathers, and another man caped as well, brilliant in 1980s Afro-funk attire. It's the chorus, and they've fixed themselves up for you. Show them some respect, y'all.)

Tommy: I have come back home, children, riding unscrupulous winds.

This amphitheater is a wreckage now. The crew is breaking down or setting up. It's hard to tell from standing here. But I do know you can't paint what ain't, and I know that everything we build falls finally into geometry. The theatre is the heart of my city, the haunt of derelicts and squirrels. It's the point of origin, the towhead in the river where the god rises out of the current and settles and takes human shape.

The whole world slopes to the stage. Behind the tiers of seating is what they call the colonnade. Stone lions guard it, and further up the hill, past Magnolia and the church and the big rock there's another statue—a girl rising up from the water like the towhead god. Hollow bronze so the Muses can hide in her

1

like Greeks in a horse. And all around me bare plywood sets, the rubble of broke mirrors catching the streetlight and bouncing it off of my sequins.

For yes, I am dressed for the occasion, children. I am afire with spangles, glittering with borrowed light.

This circuit and journey have I done, I believe. I have traveled from the forests to the south of us with their copperheads and hawks, on up through the desolations of the cement plant ruins, smokestacks like abandoned columns at the far border of the county, looking down across long expanses of smokeless tobacco shops, of auto parts stores lining one sturdy branch of highway, across tanning beds and peddler's malls until you pass beneath the interstate and the city rises up in front of you, a tangle of streets leading up to the insurance towers they rename monthly as one corporation unhinges its jaw and devours another.

Sweet homeless Jesus, it's predatory at the heights.

Makes me glad to be a man of independent means.

There's a bus stop by the university that is encased in sturdy plastic. It keeps out wind but permits the light, so it is a comfortable kind of deception. I lie there upon its benches of a night before the morning comes and arriving students might be offended by my torn and aromatic presence. From the southernmost bench, children, you can see the museum, all classical horizons and white marble like it come straight out of ancient grandeur. It is a geometry that houses blood and tears and jism. It tends toward thin air and away from our fluids and sorrows.

There is a story that I like to tell about the coins of the Roman Empire. They would mint them in Rome, at the Temple of Juno, with the emperor's profile in relief. And they say that the coins struck at Rome looked most like the man himself, but those minted in far-flung cities like Antioch, like London or Carthage, that those conjured the godly out of the profile into line and angle. The emperor's face becomes more abstract. He starts out human, and passes through icon to end up as wind and notion.

The god don't descend to stone or metal. Instead the earth shears off of him, falls away as he busts loose into space.

Which is why I rejoice when I see the museum. Imagine the god born and rising from its terrible dust, taking shape on the fired clay of pottery and the marble of the statues. Imagine all creatures on parade, bas-relief on the limestone of an old sarcophagus. It is the stage where the god first proves himself, where the god comes home.

Rise out of Italy, you girls in procession. Line the side of that flesh-eating box, and raise your lyres and scrolls and cymbals. And whether it has already happened, the god's arrival, or whether it is to come or it rises and gathers light among us now, sing to me, out of the stillness of stony dance.

2. Parodos: Strophe: Polymnia

(Manent BRISCHORDS, moving downstage left. Enter the MUSES, a chorus of nine. Dressed in short white chitons, their bare limbs dusted with marble and lime. POLYMNIA walks foremost, bearing a lyre. Of the remaining MUSES, THALIA and MELPOMENE are masked as Comedy and Tragedy respectfully, CLIO carries a scroll. TOMMY motions the Brischords to be seated, then sits among them, paying careful attention to the MUSES.)

Polymnia: It is no invocation if nobody comes when you call.

After long slumber, I am garishly lit, far from the crossroads where they first laid me to rest. Now, with all my sisters attendant, I march in frozen procession, unravished bride of quietness, daughter of memory.

Here in the museum the climate is temperate, the light bald and difficult. Here scholars, tourists, and security patrol the alcoves before the house locks down.

Under glass like latter-day Lenins, our dreams and bodies on display, we stand in marmoreal and marching order. Clio behind me, then rumpled Erato, then Euterpe and Thalia and Urania, Terpsichore dancing, and finally Kalliope and Melpomene as you would expect—all of us trooping the side of an empty sarcophagus. The stone bristles with invented life, the observers pass by, pretend to make something of this funereal lineup, this somber girls' parade.

Do they notice the trace of red where the relief wrestles out of the marble? Do they still dismiss it as rust?

I am the one all pensive and meditative, leaning across the podium as my eyes strain at stony distances. Hair bound with filet mesh, one of the two turned back to regard the progress of the others. Two of us are masked: Melpomene, all tragic and anagnoritic, grape-leafy and buskined at the tail end of things. Thalia glares at us through comic eye-holes, laughing at what things have come to, laughing that this museum might be everyone's last long tumble into night.

In the same room with us, in the same light and treated air, the deaths continue. At night, usually, but sometimes during the day. The krater—the enormous vase across from us—is older than we are. Attic and glistening, like in symposia days when it was filled with wine.

Upon it the black-figure god smiles. His bride Ariadne smiles back.

What once was tribute has fallen to artifact now, here in an American museum. They found the vessel south of Napoli and brought it here, emptied and relocated like a refugee, holding only still air and recollection. Its profiled Dionysos reclines on a couch, leering at his abandoned girl, ready to reclaim her across a shiny landscape of black and burgundy.

Of late, it was almost too late for leering. Only recently, the god had begun to die.

Melpomene noticed it first. The glister of our stone as she nodded in the direction of poor painted Bacchus. The breathy classical Greek from big sister, whispering *he is leaving us, the old drunk, old goatgluts, old prophet and piper.*

Good riddance, and I hate to see him go.

In only a short, titanic breath—in less than an hour by your reckoning—the surface of the krater began to fade, its color more blanched and ineffable, like the thought of color rather than the thing itself.

And the world is supposed to vanish along with its gods, now, isn't it?

But it won't. Nor will the gods.

You know that, despite your ingrained desire for justice or drama. You know it will go on like this until the cows and the gods come home. Until, out of the swirl of energy, all beings complete their forms.

But under glass, as I was saying. Impervious to touch. Not altogether bad, when you consider the children's disobedient fingers tracing across the breasts of the Hellenistic sculptures, and the more focused adorations of the night watchman, who caresses the louche and radiant figure of a nearby statue of the god in question, of young Dionysos, small-dicked and callipygian. I have been tempted to call out to the guard, to say to him in my inveigling Muse's accent, *Enough of that, Gus, for that is the way the god don't roll.*

Except apocryphally.

What sealed us off you will learn in due time, but we were open in early spring, free to still air and unrefracted light, only a cautionary *Do Not Touch* sign between us and fondling by bejeweled and liver-spotted hands, because who has yet seen an American heed a sign, or at least who doesn't think that somehow he is the exception to its rule?

The *he* this time was a *she*, diminutive and nervous and eighty years old at least, no doubt taking *do not touch* to be challenge rather than instruction. Guided by a heavy and exhausted son, she walked past us, extended her gloved hand and brushed a finger against Clio's scroll. Not even a pleasure sensory in such transgressions: just to have done what she did in defiance and in liberty and meanness.

We watched her leave, the infinitesimal dust on her sheathed fingertip permitting us voyage and accompaniment. For with her mischief she had given consent, she had freed us also, allowing my eyes and thoughts and pneuma and deep imagining to join her return into country she thought was safe from wandering deity.

So here is what we saw, in the Spring of the Vine and Leopard.

3. Parodos: Antistrophe: Polymnia and the Muses

Polymnia: *(Holds up a mirror)*. Be with us, Apollo Mousegetes, brother to the nine of us, as we pool in glazed *aloumínio* like lethal naiads, taking our stations beneath surface tension, watching from the rear-view mirror as Muriel's finger trails over the car's back windscreen, as she searches for evidence of dust.

Be with us as her flat brown eyes shuttle in her little fist of a face, as she insists on riding in the back seat, goes on about how her son should clean the glass, goes on against his silence.

Thalia: I love it, this front-row seat to the *théatron*, the place of viewing, where we can watch the sacrifice, the prolonged orchotomy of sons by their ancient mothers. She is good with the knife, is Muriel Thorne, and Stephen wants to drop her off before she drops his balls.

Polymnia: Now he merges on the expressway, the declining sun at his back. Riding that undercurrent of surrender he feels when he joins larger thoroughfares, as if the road he has found nurtures and buoys him, as if its history carries him toward something meaningful.

He does not not reckon on the ground beneath that same road, deep beneath concrete and rebar, visible only in the thin, exhaust-battered median. He does not reckon how in the depths of that ground, seed and root burgeon with wet life, blind as a passed-out satyr. How it shares his own receptive chemistry.

Thalia: She asks again why they had to go to the exhibit. Muriel doesn't think they are so fabulous, those museum statues. There are ones in Cave Hill just as good, she says, drooping Victorian angels in Louisville's high-end cemetery, nineteenth-century postures of kitsch and melancholy. It is her dreamed-for final destination, she reminds him.

Clio: Oh, but who will plant her there, sisters? Who, indeed, since she plans to survive her son by decades?

Thalia: *Set design,* Stephen tells her. The visit to the museum was research for a play he will direct at the park theater. When she reminds him that he is unpaid at that venue, he is quick to correct her. They pay him: admission is free.

So this *Buckeye*, she asks, has to do with old statues?

It makes me laugh.

Muriel Thorne, the old actress and mountebank, locally famous for her Medea, her Jocasta and Lady Macbeth. She very well knows the play in question, is glancing wickedly into the mirror to trammel her son's gaze. If Muriel were only attentive, she might notice me surfacing in the glass there to greet her. Instead, she self-regards, revels in the son's discomfort instead of her own facial ruin. She does not see my smirk and inspiration.

Stephen reminds his mother that she knows better. That it is *Bacchae*, not *Buckeye*. That she has the faculties to remember as much.

Muriel opens her purse to bring forth lipstick, reminding him he is a grown boy, cautioning him against silliness, wondering if Greek tragedy is not too toplofty for free entertainment.

Now Stephen sees a window between cars, and let it pass, choosing to remain in his lane. He waits, passes the next sign.

She asks if the play is ugly. If it features sex and cursing.

Stephen assures her that he will do his best to make it so.

Polymnia: Now he veers through traffic, down an exit ramp to a long accompaniment of horns and squealing brakes. Muriel looks at him, stunned, a long streak of red on her cheek and the lipstick smudged against her jaw. Accident has painted her mouth wide, like Heath Ledger's Joker's or like a sunning snake's. We laugh as Stephen smiles and heads south, gliding into one of those long, level stretches of boringly pretty old highway. The farm is on the left, the little distant stand of trees by the pond and salt lick. The drive is almost over. She can be deposited, cajoled, and left to her telephone, to right-wing radio that she claims to hate but loves because her heart indeed pumps acrimony.

What Stephen does not see—what only a goddess herself would notice, her eyes expectant on a green, half-imagined glade behind the car—is the shadow rising over the pond, indistinguishable at first from the reflection of new leaves and from the shade cast by the dip of the sun below the high hill that Stephen's car is now ascending. That darkness slowly resolves into something more solid. Dead branches, impervious to the new spring, bend before a stronger, invisible power, their reflections stirred by something surfacing into expectant dusk.

4. Parodos: Strophe: Polymnia and the Muses

(Lights rise on a bronze fountain, topped by a classical goddess, breasts bared and shimmering with the spray of water. THE MUSES surround the statue: THALIA, MELPOMENE, and CLIO join POLYMNIA downstage.)

Clio: Stephen still calls it *dope*, though *doob* for a while in the '70s. He saw the revival of *reefer*, was too white for *spliff* and *blunt*, too old for *chronic*. Almost too old for the smoke, stronger than he could have imagined in his college days, stronger also than in the paraquat-infested 70s.

Polymnia: Thunder grass: dope that creeps up on you, rumbles at your horizons, then climbs the back of your neck, sending warm consolation from your jaw to your ears and occipital, displacing you and paling the light by the courtside fountain until it becomes a summons to false bravery, a walk in the park in the dead of night when a man of 63 is subject to all dangers, from muggery to buggery to drowsing satyrs to coiled dragons guarding unspeakable treasure.

He has cast and read the yarrow stalks. The fourth hexagram, about teaching the ignorant in infancy. Something in the commentary eludes the translator—slippage in the alphabet, perhaps a tremor in the Tao.

He takes a long hit of transforming smoke and readies himself for the walk.

Clio: The court where he lives is pricey beyond his means, but close to schools and stages. His job is piecemeal, cobbled roles in local dramatic productions, directing dinner theatre. Enough to get by, for rent and for bourbon and the occasional dime bags, so that lulled by substances, he can almost believe that some turn in his life forty years ago has led to a place calm and passable.

Polymnia: Pleasantly buzzed tonight, he plugs in his old Walkman, older Zeppelin in his ears as he walks the court, the fountain at its center spotlit and glittering, the statue of the girl framed by a brace of cherubs, flourishing a bronze scarf in a cascade of water.

Clio: Galatea, they think. Who began as a statue, carved and loved into life by Pygmalion, her story receding back into bronze. Commemoration of the city's Southern Exposition of the 1880's, that celebration of a South rising out of Reconstruction. Now she stands guard as her surroundings lapse into litter and crack and property crimes, a tempest slowly compassing her affluence-protected little cove.

Polymnia: It is easy for the four of us to condense from river-valley air and soak through the tight seams of the statue, Melpomene wrestling to the hollow center of the bronze girl,

14

filling the form with divinity insubstantial, looking out through her eyes, following Stephen's gaze as it trails up and down the perfected bronze breasts and thighs like the wayward hands of museum guards.

Pygmalion himself. Rubbing bronze declivities in his thoughts, lurid to the tune of Led Zeppelin's "Houses of the Holy":

There's an angel on my shoulder, in my hand a sword of gold
Let me wander in your garden. And the seeds of love I'll sow.

Thalia and Clio and I slip into the crouching cherubs, understudies to our more theatrical sister. A city quartet. Early on you learn your part.

Clio: This theater is a tradition in this city. Ground zero and omphalos, venue for a free, uneven Shakespeare festival. Promising directors and actors make first appearances here over the years, and their promise strips away, carried off by mosquitoes and the heat of July, by an audience so inattentive that only the free seats draw them. For ten years Stephen has prowled the margins, directing and producing a play each June—amateur productions, 20th century popular fare, warm-up for the Shakespeare that people will pretend to watch.

Polymnia: No *Lear,* no *Macbeth* for our boy. Even his modest proposal of *Henry V* dismissed: he is, after all, from Louisville, and his city eats its young. So he is shuffled off to the smaller theaters, where he offers instead *The Fantasticks* and *Our Town* and *The Effect of Gamma Rays on Man-in-the-Moon Marigolds,* all of which he has come to loathe in the long Junes of the new millennium.

Thalia: Oh, don't we all, girl? But this year will be different.

Clio: Or so he says. Last December he decided to direct a huge, preposterous *Faust* for the summer season. His old friend George Castille in the title role. Devils and apes, a romance and conjury, impossible to stage much less to cast. He pitched it disastrously to the powers, who thought it was too fragmentary and hard to follow, and well, yes.

So now a *Bacchae*, kindled in stealth and beginning to flourish in his vengeful imagining. It will be fresh, he tells himself, and most of all disturbing.

Melpomene: The story, after all, is hard. King Pentheus of Thebes tries to put down the new worship of Dionysos, a cult that is turning the heads of his female subjects. Pentheus imprisons the Great God, dismisses him. For such disrespect, of course the divinity exacts revenge. Dionysos persuades the poor king to dress himself in the garb of the Maenads—the female devotees of the god. Dressed in regal drag, Pentheus may witness the sacred mysteries. Or so the god tells him as he leads the tressed and fabulous king into the mountains, handing him over to the Maenads, who tear him limb from limb.

Polýmnia: The moral is this: Imprison the god, and he returns on you with heavy duty. Push him down and press him back, stand up for *wholesomeness* and *family values* until you can't help it and the photos emerge of your meth-sotted overtures to a twelve-year-old boy in an airport restroom.

So it goes, sisters, when you can't match what you want to be with what you are. And Stephen claims no such paradox, though he has some of his own, his life contracted to bathos and mild substance abuse. Because his life is disappointing, he has concluded it is therefore authentic.

Clio: Now he takes a hit from the joint, passes the gingko tree and the landmark stone at the park entrance, and heads for the covered promenade, the slope of maples and taxus, the graveled amphitheater and the ruinous stage.

Plodding past dogwalks and picnic tables, past the upper tiers of the amphitheater, where a coterie of drunks lie sprawled and dozing, Stephen is buoyed by ambition, by lazy inspiration and THC. He waxes paunchy and prophetic as the landscape hums and receives him.

Thalia: Time to fill clothes with people, Stephen. Time to cast the play.

George Castille his usual choice, an actor ready and willing to go completely over the top in our service, tuned to our drama and happy-sad masks. He's played everyone except Godot and Lady Macbeth, even debuted a critically savaged *Hamlet* the previous summer. What the critics had not said was that Hamlet didn't play well as a fat-ass pushing seventy. So of course long-toothedness rules George out as the teenaged king and the even younger god, but Stephen will ply him with praise and merlot, wedge him into the role of Tireisias, the blind androgynous prophet twining the thyrsoi, wearing the fawn-skins, and crowning his head with ivy branches.

For the god and the tragic Pentheus, Stephen will go afield, casting his nets for youth in the high schools and community colleges, steering away from the university's drama department, where production is underway on a Noh version of *La Cage aux Folles*. There are youngsters abundant who dream of celebrity, and even if it means conversation with Dolores Starr at the high school, Stephen will brave years and resentment to reel in actors.

Polymnia: The pathway winds and silvers in front of him, like the track of a huge hunting snake. I see it all from my perch cherubic in the statue. I have a good idea where this is headed.

I slip through the seams of the putti, the Valentine Cupids, and follow the piriform figure as he wades the shadows of the park. A warm wind lofts me, upon it the whiff of blood and wine and madness. I catch him by the topmost row of the amphitheater, commingle with the cannabis and drift into his lungs, from where I might stir his speculations.

Inspiration, they call it. When they inhale the smoke of

muses, *O kapnós tou moúsa.* For the gods stalk the premises where the actors wait like statues of hollow bronze, for immortal insufflations. And ours are not the only eyes on Stephen Thorne. He knows, I can tell, by primal reliance on touch and smell. I prod his imaginations, grafting him to the tremors in the air, to the spoiled smell from the wings of the stage. In the shadows his sight is useless, but he does catch the glint of moonlight on the tomfoolery of mirrors left over from Castille's *Hamlet.* Nothing there but watery coronas spreading across the stage, tidal and bearing a feral smell, as though an animal is trapped back there, is threatened by his approach.

Stephen marks off the feeling to the drug, backs away wisely. The lights from the court beckon across a wide and deceptively tranquil bay, so he climbs back up the tiers toward the road and the fountain and the brightness. He remembers ascending the stairs from the cellar of the old house he and Muriel had rented in the South End back in the '50s, how he took the topmost steps with a long stride, a runner's gait, imagining the darkness rushing behind him like an entangling current ...

Yes, I know what he remembers, inveigled as I am in his lungs and motherwit. For who but Memory is my mother, when all is said and done? *Mnemosyne, μητέρα μούσες.* Mother of Muses.

Stephen breathes much more easily under the first streetlamps, his heart rising as his lungs prickle in the humid spring night, and exhaled, I slide free of definition, swallowed by a darkness in which my senses recover clarity and focus, in which I join my masked sisters, intent on the stage and its attendant derelicts.

Back in the park, the Boss lies snoring on the topmost tier, covered in a dismantled cardboard box and pages of the Sunday *Courier,* stinking of Richards and stale piss.

Melpomene: You should have let me at dear Stephen. I would have permeated his heaviness, sent him home gibbering with visions of the infernal Styx...

Polymnia: Girl, you are eat up. Practice on the Boss.

Thalia: And so the aethereal leavening begins. Melpomene hovers above the hulking, lamé-clad T. Tommy Briscoe, the park's resident pervert and flaneur, self-appointed Boss of the Midnight Choir. She slides down his throat, lamenting the malodor of his breath as she draws him toward wakening. T. Tommy stirs, then, his lamé refulgent, sitting upright and speaking in no tongue this Muse has heard as his entourage approaches from the shadows, gathering substance from the clammy air.

5. Parodos: Antistrophe: T. Tommy Briscoe and the Brischords

(Manent THE MUSES, moving upstage left, as T. TOMMY BRISCOE and THE BRISCHORDS move into the light, downstage center. TOMMY spreads his cape on the stage gently, sits on it, as THE BRISCHORDS encircle him.)

T. Tommy: One of the Gifts of the Holy Spirit, they tell us, is the gift of tongues. Another of them gifts the interpretation of said speaking in tongues.

Gather around me, children, for another revelation.

Here. Up on the stage. Stay away from them mirrors, Daddy Chrome, and stop looking at your mullet, which like Jesus is with you always: business in front, party in the back.

I know the fat man come too close to us. I know, DJ Mel,

that all we need is some pot-smoking fucker to get in trouble, to run into us, and you know they won't let us stay here then, that we'll be forced into the shelters or something worse…

But he ain't coming back. Not just yet. So tarry a while.

Listen to what he took away with him. Zepp's "Kashmir"— the lurch and *ritardando* of Page's guitar, riding the wind off the hilltop. That dark surge before Plant lays down the vocals over it. Squirrels in the overhead branches, birds up in the balcony where Lady Macbeth was unsexed by spirits intent on mortal thoughts, where the old invert caught a glimpse of himself in a mirror and imagined his father's ghost, imagined himself all Prince of Denmark.

Listen to the ground doves break cover, and listen backstage where the old boy stirs.

Brischords: *To sit with elders of the gentle race, this world has seldom seen. They talk of days for which they sit and wait, all will be revealed.*

T. Tommy: Can I get a witness? The assent, the *uh-huh* of the Jordanaires, like they sung behind the King?

Y'all are my Brischords, children. Join in the revelry.

Brischords: *Oh, father of the four winds, fill my sails, across the sea of years…*

T. Tommy: It's like that, the speaking in tongues. They make up words that sound pretty. Because there is no language for that strong blind current, that gust of wind that bears along our rudderless boats. We stand on deck and watch. We interpret, but we don't translate. And by the time we interpret, it sounds like something we wanted to hear all along. It becomes what we expected, and it shores up our main hope, children, our hope that we don't have to change nothing on account of what it told us. My body is a ship, is flowing water, my hair a winding current, tangled up in high grass and brilliantine.

I've been here through thirty Thunders and a Curfew Law, through busing riots and a tornado. I toured with the Doors and played the Fairgrounds on Halloween Night. I row-boated through the suburbs as the Ohio swelled in '63. And the waters flow into earlier waters, back before all your times, and I remember despite myself the whole town sinking in '37 as I headed to the Highlands ahead of the cresting river…

And it is only a step from that flood to another tornado, back to the Exposition and back farther, to the whiff of an antique war, hurdling flood and tempest and flood again, and farther back to the youth of the god, to a soft boy drinking with Aristaios on a hillside that was and was not Kentucky, to honey commingling with wine and youth with age as the two reclined drunkenly…

The Exposition. And why in the fuck am I remembering an Exposition, a hundred and god damned twenty years ago?

Believe me or don't. It ain't that I'm lying, but that the truth gets diverted when it passes through me.

It's partly the smell of this place, I promise. The odor from the theatre. I caught a whiff of it this morning while I watched from in the wings, rubbing one out over them spandexed girls on the sidewalk. Half-coppery reptile stank making me stop in mid-contemplation.

The Southern Exposition. Reptiles in untended ground.

Great blistered mother of the god if they ain't back.

Brischords: *Te senior turpi sequitur Silenus asello*
Turgida pampineis redimitaus tempora sertis….
Vae puto archetypus fio.

T. Tommy: I think…I am fixing to become an archetype.

THE BRISCHORDS help TOMMY to his feet. They move downstage right.

6. Episode: The Origins of Stephen Thorne

(Exeunt TOMMY and BRISCHORDS. POLYMNIA and THE MUSES move center.)

Polymnia: He claims to be Orpheus, torn apart by women.

But it is more complex than Stephen imagines. Women and country and self-rending all conspired to leave him tattered.

Precocious and indulged son of a mother too smart for the good of either of them, he was Muriel Thorne's performer and trophy in his early years. He was gold, salvaged from a wrecked marriage and abandoning father, reciting random passages from plays, films, and television shows. He was precocious from the time he could talk, a smart child but by no means the immortal that Muriel imagined in her fantasy: he was no god to erase all indignity, to carry his mother out of the dark netherworld in yet another predictable rescue story.

Muriel knew as much by the time he graduated high school, but Stephen did all right for his nurture. He graduated somewhere near the head of his class because the standards were low and nobody took that well to reading in his sports-besotted school, or in his community, for that matter. Only one other in his class headed to college out of state, and Stephen went there with relief, left Kentucky and shook the dust from his feet, bound for the East and drama school, where his mother's early delusions had pointed him before she gave up and turned back to thinking about herself.

He arrived in the fall of '67, joining an incoming class of indulged, lazy children, their talents also magnified by doting parents.

They would change the world like rock musicians.

And it was here Stephen was found out, unmasked like a dropped disguise in an old comedy: he was clever, pretty much, in things he should have outgrown by eleven or twelve, or should have pressed further, into something deeper and wiser. And though Yale Drama was neither all that deep nor all that wise, it took only a term to weed him out, to transplant him back into harsh country, into his native ground, hard as tombstones for the genuine article, but arable enough to fool most anyone else.

His bus left New Haven in early '68, harbored in the disappointment of every mother.

Kent was a kind of halfway house when Stephen arrived the next September. Muriel let it be known, lets it be known unto this day, as if her listeners care, the strings she pulled somewhere in the vast theatrical fabric to get him admitted to the program. Before he could thank her, Stephen was on the bus to Ohio, sure and forever to be reminded that he was salvaged by his mother's efforts. This time an education degree, because, as she reminded him, *those who can't, teach.*

He stalked the margins of Kent State's Theatre Arts program.

Auditioned for *Streetcar* and *Death of a Salesman*, worked the lights for a local production of *The Music Man.* Sat perplexed in the audience of an Alternative People's Theatre as the first *Bacchae* he'd ever seen proved to him that *alternative* sometimes means *god-awful.* Still, the Passion of Isaac Clarke, as he came to call it later, has lain fallow in his thoughts until home country and this summer forty years after.

In later years he has told of brushes with famous afterthoughts. When everyone was talking *Thomas Covenant the Unbeliever*, Stephen remembered long talks with its author, though in truth only once did he think he saw the man, at a distance on that hill by the architecture building. And when the Next Generation of *Star Trek* came out—the Next Generation, not the one with Kirk and Spock—Stephen siphoned hipness from two magnified conversations with Jon De Lancie, and his students' eyes widened because, as he had found, teenage drama students believe most anything.

But he did know Sandra Scheuer, if only in his thoughts. Dark hair, and as he recollected her, a late-'60s-yearbook kind of pretty, though his nostalgia and his story might have magnified her beauty. She studied speech therapy, but maybe he read that somewhere. And in the aftermath everyone discovered how little the war involved her, though she was against it in a vague and gentle fashion.

Later he imagines her as his girlfriend. He imagines her standing at the edge of another knoll, in a park three hundred miles and forty years from Kent.

Stephen had slept in on that Monday morning. Woke up to the sound of what they had come to call the Victory Bell. The Guardsmen had been there since April 30 or May 1, or at least that was how he remembered it. He followed the ringing, made his way up the south side of the hill by the architecture building. As he got almost half way up, following the wall, the Guard came up the other side and crested the hill. Some of them squatted down so the others behind them could shoot over their heads. One of them trained his gun on Stephen. He could not see the

27

man's face for the gas mask.

Then the column turned, fired at something behind Taylor Hall. The Guardsman took his gun off Stephen, and the line of armed men began to stir around. Stephen had to walk right by them, and he smelled upon them their psychic disarray, although this part he would forget later, forget that they were swept along in the same current, the weight of what they did sinking no doubt, to a deep and alien bed.

So he gave dimes to two girls, who rushed off to call for ambulances. Then he looked down at the parking lot beside Prentice Hall, where someone sprawled on the pavement, a stunned group of students circling her.

Later, he imagined himself closer to Sandra. Present at the moment of her passing, at the loss of light in her eyes, though he was not there and he was too late for that veiled and quiet intimacy. And he was even more removed in the days to come. For although he did not know it in May of 1970, Stephen Thorne had begun to leave the campus.

7. Episode: Of Returns and Classroom Scandals

Polymnia: By now it would be hard to tell Stephen that he did not know the girl, that at most he met her only in passing or in memory or in dreams.

As Sandra Scheuer passed into myth, Stephen tumbled from job to job, from record shops and bookstores to Fotomat and Convenient, waiting in the meadow for a light to develop out of events. Eventually he saw that waiting was not enough to evoke the wondrous. So he came back to Louisville in the fall of 1973.

He was caught in the current now. Now it was the god that marshaled him. Stephen only had to watch where he was headed and to believe that watching mattered and would help him.

By the time Bicentennial came around, he was teacher-certified and working. His mother praised him on the outside and hated him inwardly. After all, he had traded in her large dreams: he was teaching English and Drama in high school, up in a third-floor classroom directing the Senior Play. The long flow of the godly river had turned to a bourgeois trickle.

Stephen pretended he was all right with it. Now and then when he couldn't sleep, he thought that it was best for him, that careers in the bona fide were for those for whom the dice fell. He should be pleased with where he was ending up, he told himself on those nights. He should cast things into the comfort of past tense.

But all the while he was miring himself deeper, until the god's rescue could come only through violence.

She was sixteen and Dolores Webb at the time: not all that attractive, but thin and blonde and disastrous for a man who yearned for female attentions. She was eager in his drama class, quick to the major role in his production of *Our Town* (she shared the last name of the character she played; only he seemed to notice). Dolores seemed the perfect promising student until a policeman's casual flashlight sweep of idling cars at a park overlook discovered teacher and student intertwined, Dolores in dishabille, Stephen with his pants opened and dismantling his career in the act of cupping her firm and exposed little buttocks.

Suspension first. Then dismissal, and the two of them shrank into exile. Stephen left the school and went back to small supporting roles at the Iroquois Amphitheater musicals, a brief stint as a part-time clerk at Dry Salvages, the city's alternative bookstore, then moving in with Muriel, who was appalled by everything. Dolores went through the motions until her graduation. The couple saw each other secretly while the scandal persisted and the Webb family threatened legal action, then on and off several years more. They parted for good, and in no friendly fashion, on stage.

Here is what happened. Stephen had received a job offer at the local community college, an adjunct drama coach under the command and direction of George Castille. Castille, was an actor of some talent who had never risen above his city, playing bit roles regionally and larger roles at home. He was one of those artists who grew to middling size in a small pond: it helped to be born somewhere in Illinois, because Louisvillians had all decided you couldn't be any good and be born here. So George had his exotic origins, and he could also charm and strongarm in a way that mimicked what the gods dispense.

If you did not look too closely, you would think he was better than he was. And Stephen did not look closely at first. George was obviously homosexual, and if it had taken flirting a little, taken anything just short of actual congress, Stephen might have gone that way for a theatre job. But George simply wanted an assistant director. Stephen even wondered whether he should be insulted, but he jumped at the job.

And Dolores was jumping at her own good fortune. She enrolled at once at the same school, figuring she had worked the casting couch already. There would be roles for her, she was certain. Ophelia or Isabella or even Medea. The dreaming fell short when they staged *Our Town* again, and Stephen passed her over for the same Emily Webb role she had played in high school. She auditioned, played the motions and emotions, only to see other girls' names on the call-back sheet George Castille posted two weeks before the first readings began.

She blamed Castille. Took her whine to Stephen and found out otherwise. Why he owned up to it is anyone's guess, but maybe it was just the moment when a man comes clean because dragging the world down with you beats living in the world that's up and running.

It marked the last act of Thorne and Webb. For a while Dolores got to play a kind of Medea, majored on the *hell hath no fury*. She wedged notes in the door of Stephen's small office, going on about her solitude, her isolation, his broken pledges and her lost innocence, hinting at backlash and vengeance.

One afternoon, locked in the office, Stephen watched as her silhouette passed across the far side of the door's frosted glass, as she pressed her face against it, trying vainly to see inside. He held his breath and wished for complete silence.

She was a girl possessed, willing to lay all things at the altar of her vengeance. If her child had been born, she would have sacrificed him then and there.

But Stephen was in the hands of the god by now, protected and guided. And our sister Erato, most immodest of the Muses, found another man, a modest one, to catch the eye of Dolores Webb and to haul in her suspect sanity. This was a seminary student, an idealist who took up some of the time between Stephen and the Robert Starr she would marry five years later. Because Dolores was transformed by loves, on her way from wronged woman to anti-muse, serial companion to disappointments. Perhaps she pitched in with the failure.

So all along, up to this spring night in the park, Stephen had been dodging the thunderbolt. The god had reserved a place for him.

But immortal attention is rarely the best of things.

8. Episode: Of Returns and Imagined Scandals

Polymnia: *Hold to him in truth and loyalty,* the I Ching tells him. Advice of half the readings, but heeded this time, in a convergence of need and old connection. Still, it was hard to return here, to the scene of his transgressions.

George Castille had been the wise one. Masking all things sexual, steering away from high schools. Visiting only to audition for youthful parts, curbing himself to the teacher's lounge, its vending machines and clandestine ashtrays. It was safer that way in a city like this, a metropolitan area of nearly a million but at its heart a church-haunted small town where innocent conversations could flow right into witch-hunts. Today George would be at the school, only because Stephen had asked him to join the production.

The teachers' lounge lies down the long central hall, and

Stephen passes by rows of paint-thickened, khaki-colored lockers, expecting a band of maenads or Iroquois to burst forth, through whom he would have to run a gauntlet. It hasn't dawned on him yet that only George and Dolores Webb—Dolores Starr, he reminded himself—would remember a scandal from thirty-five years back. A man likes to cut a wicked figure, and he is a bit disappointed when the facts dawned on him.

He has almost settled to the task at hand when Dolores comes out from her classroom and regards him in what he half hopes is still a hostile light.

The hexagram had said:

> *Truth, like a full earthen bowl:*
> *Thus in the end*
> *Good fortune comes from without.*

And "Dolores," Stephen says. "Dolores. How are you?"

"What brings you here, Stephen?" she asks. "Drama or dalliance?"

Stephen tries smiling. "Is there a third choice?"

Dolores has strength enough to carry grudges. Nor is she too much worse for wear outwardly. Blonde hair tends to resist gray, and only her nose suffers the droop and distention of years, that drying in their forties that makes thin women look like apple dolls.

Stephen sticks to business, explains what had brought him to the school, smiles and asks after her son (though he does not care, not really), hoping Dolores will take the lure.

"Aron? Aron's well, thank you for asking," she says. "Talented, but a bit green as an actor. To be expected at his age. Still, I wouldn't be surprised if George has him in mind for a role in your little production."

Everything in such a statement bothers him. How Dolores moves from authority to co-conspirator to supplicant in five sentences. But Stephen draws the most friction from her calculated use of *little*. "There are no little productions, Dolores. You know the saying," he replies aridly. And then, because he

34

could: "The part of Agave is still open, by the way. Greek tragedy always has plum roles for middle-aged women, you know. Men played them first."

She wishes him icily well as the bell rings. Slipped back into her classroom, right behind a straggling pair of students in letter jackets. Stephen wonders that boys still wear those things, then wades through loitering scholars on his way to Castille and the lounge.

He does the math on Aron, and it still works out. The kid took his stepfather's name when Dolores rushed into the one connection that ended in marriage, bad as Stephen has heard it was. Everyone had guesses as to the boy's sire, but Aron was what? seventeen? eighteen at the oldest?

Stephen is clear by at least a decade. He still can't pin down why he went through the counting.

9. Episode: Of Returns and Invented Scandals

Polymnia: George Castille sits in a corner of the lounge, smoking Winstons and offering the opinion that *The Bacchae* won't fly this summer.

Stephen tries wishing away the silk bandanas and the clip-on earring, but Castille delights in playing to an audience, flaming the old school with safe effrontery.

He may not have been a great actor, but he is still good enough to scandalize his public.

"If it was up to me, Stephen, and *purely* up to me," he booms, gesturing with the cigarette, "I would say, 'have at it, and goddamn the consequences.'"

Two of the younger teachers, seated by a vending machine, look up at the *goddamn* from their conversation about *peer review* and *planning periods* and students named Harris and Rausch.

Stephen lowers his voice, hoping to set better tone and volume, but George isn't having it.

"You know what they're like here, Stephen. Nothing will be said about it, because the Festival directors are all professed liberals and freedom-of-expression types. You know: 'We'll fight for your right to say *piss* because it's justified by the plot and character.' Makes them feel good. They can go home and listen to NPR without that nagging sense of uselessness. But they won't let you do it. It's too risky for the limousine types out east."

"I'm going to do *The Bacchae*, George. And you know they'll back me on it. It's Euripides, for God's sake."

"Euripides, Eumenides, like the old Greek woman told her tailor son. It's classic as it comes, I'll grant you, but there's sex and cross-dressing, honey, and what's more, it's theologically… unkempt. No Protestant Jesus to step in and make things right. It's the twenty-first century, where we burn ancient homos and heretics in the board rooms. You'll make it worse for grants and donations with your pagan romp, and who knows? I might have been intending to exhume my critically acclaimed *Hamlet* next summer."

He rolls his eyes, snuffed the cigarette and produced another, offering the packet as usual to Stephen. Who declines, as usual.

The young teachers back out of the lounge, whispering.

"I'm set in my ways, George," Stephen allows. "And I know I've almost outlasted you on this, or you wouldn't be here. I'm more stubborn in my declining years, I suppose."

"Oh, aren't you, though! That's why I'll be the better human being, though you will have casting problems as well. I don't know any good amateur Agaves, and I'd shudder to make a teen-aged girl crouch and crone in the role."

"I broached it to Dolores on the way in. She seemed not taken."

George chuckles. "It's because you have a way with her, Stephen. She is still Emily Webb when she looks in the mirror, though everyone else is seeing *Myrtle* Webb, for God's sake. Her son, by the way, is not a horrid actor. I've used him in minor speaking parts at the college, and I'll arrange for you to talk to him. Dolores knows, and has given her consent. He's a little heavy and pouty, but he'd make a passable young god."

"She knew then? So *that* was a show of forgiveness? An attempt to drop her offspring into my play?"

George pushes his Palin eyeglasses down the bridge of his nose and peered at his old friend over the lenses. "Beware, good Stephen," he warned ironically. "You're still the cloudiest one of us all."

10. Episode: Night of the Panther

(THE MUSES emerge from the shadow to center stage, encircle POLYMNIA. ERATO, white chiton disheveled, left breast almost pruriently free of the garment, stands behind POLYMNIA, playfully propping her chin on her sister's shoulder.)

Polymnia: In fact, Dolores knows she has absolved Stephen Thorne. She has no idea when she did so, because it involved no conscious act of will, this forgiveness, but was simply a branch of the current that has taken her to where she is, to a vantage point from which she sees him as disheveled and dumpy and graying and in need of amnesty.

   In the hall she plays the role of wronged, deflowered girl, because it is a role worth playing and because it plays young, and she enjoys the freshness of it, the drama and the conviction that makes Stephen feel guilty and uneasy. She sees it in his eyes, and nourishes herself on the look. But she knows that he has come to choose another player for another role, and she hopes it will be Aron, and that for his first principal role, her son will play a god.

Leaning against the locker she yearns for a drink, but feels peace with the direction of things.

Dolores knows that there are speculations as to Aron's father. Nobody thought it was Ronnie Starr, a ne'er-do-well smelling of graft and pomade, who passed through her life shortly after the boy's birth, leaving the scarcest of ripples and a surname to remind her she had not imagined a husband.

And a former husband is good, anchoring and almost respectable. Back in the early 90s, unmoored and marginal, Dolores Webb had imagined the Night of the Panther.

ERATO steps forward, kisses POLYMNIA's cheek fondly, and continues the story.

Erato: Living alone in a cottage, a long commuter's ride from her first job as a teacher's aide, Dolores had battened on ice cream and cheap Chablis, a solitary existence that time and again pushed her from melancholy to near crazy. She rationed her cartons of Winston Lights, watched television with reception on only two channels, and listened to Prince and Duran Duran until her thoughts whelmed with sadness and lust and failed promise.

It was one of those nights, buzzed but not yet drunk on the wine, she sat on the porch in a temperate spring and heard a coughing sound, a tremor of bushes from the copse beside the driveway. The cat emerged from the shadow and stood on the moonlit crest of her yard, its eyes calm and alien. Dolores' first shock at seeing a predator on her lawn subsided into curiosity, then under its gaze, into a strange, removed serenity of her own. She clutched her open dress in the front, recalling the story of some disastrous, feral attack on a girl in these parts fifty years, a century ago. Decided it did not matter. Rose and stumbled in the rising, then surprisingly steady for wine, she drifted over the silvered grass as the animal, lowering its front legs almost submissively, approached her with the pivoting gait of a jungle creature, which she knew it was not, could not be.

Its muzzle smelled of fresh blood, was crusted and sticky

against her neck as Dolores cradled the big head. The eyes were glittering, opaque, and filled with a deep, heart-rending intelligence that might have been the animal's nature or simply her own imagining. She should have been afraid, she thought later, but not now, the moment passing tidally over her, over both of them, as borne on an impulse she would write off later as a dream provoked by alcohol, she slid onto the ground, her arms around the creature's neck, her legs spreading as she lifted her skirt, raised her legs and surrendered to a heat that entered her and grew.

Polymnia: Sister, dear sister. This is impossible to stage.

Erato: As if we planned to stage this. It's a play for voices at best, girl. At worst, a novel.

> (*She glares at the audience*).

And not a word from any of you about "worst".
Now leave me be.
In the morning, covered in dew in the uncut grass, Dolores was shamed by her dreaming. Dreams are unaccountable, she thought. You cannot shape them out of the wild subterranean rivers from which they arise. As the years and wine bottles passed, she would forget this compromise, this lapse of her sentinels, only to think of it six, seven summers later, after a long sentence of celibacy and solitude, when she missed the monthly bleeding and went, after the second month, to her doctor, a kind and discreet old general practitioner, who, along with Dolores Webb, was the first to wonder the name of the man who had fathered the child in her womb.

Polymnia: For a while she stood over Aron's crib at night, trying to conjure maternal instinct and coming up with anxiety. Wished it was fear for the child. *That* fear would somehow be motherly. Instead, she recognized it as a kind of haunting, like the one she had felt on the moon-spangled grass of her lawn. Aron seemed like a changeling, sullen in his bassinette. Still, she wanted to keep him as her shrine's guardian, to keep him a boy always.

There was menace in the nightly vigils. Hard to bear while thinking well of yourself. So as the boy grew, Dolores pushed the memories under and fashioned more suitable ones, ones in which she brushed back the soft hair from the infant's face and they both played the roles acceptable: he the god in the cradle, and she both his proper and foster mother.

11. Episode: The Game Begins

(ERATO steps back into the shadows, still visible, though, at the edge of the light. Manet POLYMNIA, who produces a red glass polyhedron, displays it for the audience.)

Polymnia: The glitter of jewels on the table. Rare harvest from Asian mines. Resolving into dice, into what my sisters and I call *tesserae, astragali…*
knucklebones.
The hoard of Aron Starr, who awaits his comrades and writes mysteries in a spiral notebook.
He looks less exotic than his mother lets on. Dark hair from the reputed father—whether Ronnie Starr indeed or some mysterious interloper—and a physique that tends toward the stocky rather than the heavy. Prominent nose, small brown eyes with a hint of sneak and calculation. The features of a character actor.

He awaits his friends—Apache Downs, Billy Shepard, and the De Chevre twins—for the game the lot of them play every Tuesday night, ritual in its regularity and course of action.

The dice lie scattered on papers, on old and clumsily illustrated books, on a map superimposed with geometric grids. Unlikely materials giving rise to story—a chain of fragments and episodes, linked together only by sequence. Each one present at the table breathes life in and through the mask of a character. In Aron's game, they take on Nordic roles—Tolkien roles—of knight or wizard, elf or dwarf, to participate in an imagined world over which Aron Starr is a good-natured god. Part drama, part myth, part community of souls, the story flows from player to player like divinity through the hands of the poets.

There are students more polished and popular who think these Tuesday nights and role-playing games are trivial and sad. But this group who assembles in Aron's basement is not the general band of adolescent nerds and outcasts.

Though Apache Downs plays close to type.

Along with the benign and sparse-bearded Billy Shepard, Apache is Aron's classmate, named by hippie parents, christened into general strangeness from an early age. He hulks over video games and SF movie listings, dresses as a Star Wars rebel for the conventions. Even learns manufactured languages—Klingon, of course, Dothraki, and Sindarin Elvish.

Neither he nor Billy, though, figures much in what will happen. They are secondary characters, tributaries, Rosencrantzes and Guildensterns to the thing of the play.

The De Chevre twins, on the other hand, are older, physically beautiful and more gifted. Aron had noticed Maia at once, two years ahead of him at the high school, blonde, radiant, and unattainable. Vincent is, in his own way, as lovely as his sister: the same golden cascade of hair and the sorcery of hazel eyes. It is no accident that Maia plays a magic-user in the game and her brother a druid: witchery paces before them, and hearts bow down to one, or the other, or in some cases both.

Apache plays a fighter, and Billy a thief. And Aron governs

it all, for the idea behind such games is that the players assume roles in a fictional setting, the story unfolding according to the decisions they make and the chance element of dice rolls. In short, it is an improvisational drama that one of the players, the game master, plans out, directs and umpires.

Aron's game centers on a rescue. The party of characters have set out to rescue the heir to a mythical kingdom, a prince ensorcelled and trapped in an underground labyrinth. Aron's four friends—Apache and Billy, Maia and Vincent—form the core of the adventuring party. Sometimes others join the game, dipping in and out of the story in cameo appearance, their importance fleeting and slight.

But nothing is trivial on this Tuesday night, for Billy Shepard brings with him a young man he had met at the Antioch Baptist Church where his parents worship and he sits and bides his time through tedious Biblical passages and sermons. Jack Rausch was the most interesting creature to pass through the doors of Antioch, and Billy had known it instantly. So this night, pleased with his coup of friendship, he introduces Jack to the band of friends.

Apache is neither interested nor impressed, but Vincent and Maia take up with the new boy immediately, as Billy had nine days before, in the austere sanctuary stripped of raiment and metaphor, where Jack Rausch had been serene and grinning, attentive to the Reverend Peter Koenig, his gaze meandering from the pulpit to the Plexiglas windows and the dreaming landscape outside.

See? Billy whispers to Maia, having made introductions, as Aron briefs Jack on how to create his character, the six rolls of three dice that would determine his strength, intelligence, wisdom, dexterity, and charisma—the basic attributes that, under the game rules, governed all characters as fundamentally as chromosomes.

See, Maia? I told you this guy is awesome!

Aron is unconvinced. He has yearned after Maia for a year now, has tried to ply Vincent's help in the suit through various briberies. The twins have been friendly, but not in the way Aron wants. Here, within fifteen minutes, he sees the strong, tidal pull of Jack Rausch. Both De Chevres play up to the new boy, laugh too loudly at his consciously clumsy ignorance of the game rules. Flirt with him as he made the preliminary dice rolls.

All of the rolls are high. Baffling odds. Two times the rolls max out—three sixes, one in 216 chance individually, and taken together, slipping toward a math Aron cannot negotiate without paper and a calculator. It is dismally appropriate that Jack should be blessed.

Aron shrinks into his chair, reading the text that will prompt the evening's play. Jack's eyes are on him—eager, amiable, intent.

The rest of the players are looking at Jack.

12. Episode: The Foundling

(POLYMNIA steps back among THE MUSES, takes THALIA's mask, and moves back to center stage. She puts on the mask and speaks through its abstract grin.)

Polymnia: It comes down to a question of origins. Jack Rausch is darkly handsome and slim, Asian and feline of feature, very different from the burly Germanic Rausches, and resembling the Congressman only those who are looking for resemblances can see.

The Indiana House of Representatives is a respectable body, and the Republican majority of that house is postured even more respectably: legally obedient and publicly asexual. So when Beverly Nguyen, the young, unwed campaign worker for Roy Rausch, began to show in what was apparently the fourth month of her pregnancy, it would, of course, mark the end of her work for the candidate. She was sent back to her people—Vietnamese immigrants living in a large extended-family crowd under one small roof in New Albany. And in most cases, her story would have ended when she left.

But Roy Rausch confided to his campaign manager, Bucky Trabue, the girl's enticements, the light blouses she had purposefully worn in a warm and humid May and how the fan at headquarters had stirred the fabric, how she reached for the topmost shelf and the pamphlets, her hips contraposed and how he watched, bedazzled and helpless, from the amen corner. And how things moved in a way that Roy Rausch claimed and claimed was inevitable until Bucky, a shrewd veteran of more than right-wing political campaigns, recognized it for what it was. And *oh, no, Roy,* he objected, *oh surely not, the kid's barely of age and you're married and every Baptist preacher in the district has endorsed you, and after all, she's Vietnamese, for the love of God...*

At his desk that evening Bucky welsh-combed his thinning hair, drank the syrupy leavings of the morning's coffee and speculated on how fucking tired he was of covering the tracks of men who talked like Republicans and acted like Democrats. The campaign might keep it veiled, he guessed, unless Adele Rausch found out.

The Queen Bee. Adele, Whose Hand is Above. The one who wanted her husband Roy in prominent political office, and finding him forty-two and behind schedule, had hired campaign manager, staff, and a dozen workers, nine of whom were males and the other three safely post-menopausal. She rode mistrust as roughshod as ambition, and all it would take was one loose set of lips on the staff, one breath stirring that she could get wind of...

Bucky suspected it was no longer a matter of days but of hours.

So to New Albany he went, and spoke to the girl herself because the parents' English was broken and no amount of slowing down or speaking louder seemed to make them understand. Beverly, on the other hand, was fluent and smart, and Bucky hoped to Jesus she was as old as she said she was when she signed on with the campaign. And no, when she asked him point blank, he couldn't guarantee her safety or that of her child, and couldn't compromise a clear Republican principle by sending her to the Women's Clinic in Louisville, because Jesus Christ on a pony if that got into the presses it would mean not only the Rausch campaign but his own career forever and ever, so yes, Miss Beverly Nguyen it was time to get the hell out of town and lie low till the most murderous of notions had passed through Adele Rausch and through Roy's three older sisters.

At his departure, Beverly Nguyen's concern rose quickly to panic. As Bucky drove west toward home, lighting his second rationed cigarette of the evening and wondering if he had dodged the bullet (or better yet, had taken it without injury for Roy Rausch), Beverly's brother Sammy had jump-started the family's Mercury Cougar, a car older than the girl who would ride in it, clicking on what the Nguyens had thought was its third hundred-thousand of miles when in fact it was its fourth, the odometer having been rolled back by one Lyle Trabue, Bucky's cousin over in Jeffersonville, in a misdeed completely unconnected to Rausch, Bucky, or any political campaign in southern Indiana, but just indicative of human nature.

And Beverly, carrying a secret so veiled that the one Bucky suspected was obvious and even comical, afraid of being spotted leaving town, afraid Adele Rausch already knew and was sending disreputable henchmen in revenge, climbed into the trunk and, over Sammy's more sensible protests, persuaded her brother to tie the door back down and drive them toward Madison, where their aunt had promised a refuge. Jack Rausch would claim later that the first thing he remembered was that darkness, the smell of oil and the bump of tires on the state road.

And young Beverly Nguyen singing, soothing her newborn child with an old Paul McCartney lullaby.

The Muses: *Golden slumbers fill your eyes*
Smiles awake you when you rise
Sleep pretty darling do not cry
And I will sing a lullabye…

Polymnia: …neither of them ever knowing the words were three centuries older.

But Jack claimed, and his mother confirmed, that as her sweet thin voice moved from chorus to verse, as she held the baby she could not protect and as she wondered how she could give him up, *if* she could give him up, that her singing broke on the first line of the verse:

Once there was a way…to get back homeward.

And for two years, somewhere to the east of all of these things, there was no way to return.

13. Episode: Taken In

(POLYMNIA returns the mask to THALIA, who moves upstage with the rest of THE MUSES, into the shadows. POLYMNIA remains in the light, faces the audience.)

Polymnia: The baby on the doorstep. The foundling child whose promise is miraculous, heroic.

In the city, Dolores darkened as Aron failed to live up to legend, but across the river, in the ancestral house of the Rausches, a baby showed up and sparked mythological ambitions in the family.

The three Rausch sisters thought of Moses, of course, but there were others: Oedipus, Perdita, Snow White and Tom Jones. And though the sisters were not famous for warmth or safe harbor, it was a vein of kindness—too far submerged to be visible but there nevertheless—that prompted them to take the baby in.

That, and the simple fact that they had seen it coming.

The Rausch sisters were no longer Rausch in name, but only in allegiance. Theirs was a prominent family, and the girls had insisted on homes within a block of each other, on frequent visits that became eventually constant. You would find them together in the ancestral parlor, playing cards, watching television, comparing shopping coups and husbandly achievements. As they reached their thirties, their marriages, thin to begin with, fell into more private dissolutions. Now one was widowed, two divorced, and all three convergent on their ancient and formidable matriarch, Madeline Rausch of Indiana Republican circles, wealthy and unable to suffer foolery unless it was her own. Which she, of course, had relabeled eccentricity, and was probably right.

Madeline was the only one who recognized on the baby the lineaments of Roy Rausch, the oldest and most highly regarded of her children. She remembered the conversations with Bucky Trabue (whom she loathed but respected), and knew that her one choice was to accept the infant. She gave out rumors that her youngest daughter, the respectably widowed Ina, had chosen to adopt a child of Asian heritage. Ina obeyed without hesitation, and Jack Rausch was raised by an aunt whom he called mother while knowing otherwise.

The girls claimed that the child had no Rausch in him.

Madeline's will overruled them all.

Madeline thought of the child as a changeling. Once, when Jack was no more than three, she watched him at play in Ina's room, serenely sorting old costume jewelry into piles according to a pattern Madeline sensed was there but veiled by the child's age or some great distance he had already traveled away from this nest of women.

Jack looked up at his grandmother, who thought she would fancy him beautiful if he were less her own. And "Maddaw," he said, his smile almost radiant, the jewelry (she swore) catching sun from the window and glittering in his brown hands like something more than paste and glass, as though his touch itself transformed it into gems.

She was "Maddaw" to him. She had corrected him when he called her "Grandma" or (even more horribly) "Mammaw". He was to call her Madeline, as did her other two grandsons.

54

But little Jack blurred the lines of custom, and as irritating as she sometimes found him, Madeline knew this was the one whose affinities were most her own.

He revealed himself as she watched him in secret, as he had with the gems. At first she thought Jack's unobserved play was a window into who he really was. But instead, she noticed that he played to an audience as though he sensed her eyes.

When he was five, Madeline found him at the roll-top desk in the parlor, arranging Italian postcards in a ragged circle. She approached him almost stealthily, her soft steps masked by his lovely, atonal humming. The cards were the photos from the Villa of the Mysteries, a sequence of interior murals that portrayed the life of the god Dionysos, and Madeline took in her breath to see them arranged in their proper order, each frescoed scene leading to the next, as they did on the walls of the villa.

The guides had told her it probably marked an initiation—a death and rebirth for young women. That it probably told the story of the god and his bride Ariadne, the girl abandoned by a fickle lover on the island of Naxos, who slept the sleep of the dead or dying until the god himself found her, and like the prince in the fairy tale, kissed her into life and wedlock. Because, of course, life and wedlock were much the same thing for some Roman girls, but Madeline had lost interest once the story was told.

But this time, she heard the story differently. The child's stubby fingers pointed to figures in the photos, renaming them and retelling their stories. Suddenly, the sleeping Ariadne became *mama*, though whether that referred to Ina, to the vanished Beverly Nguyen, or to Madeline herself was unclear.

She sat down by him, drew out the story. She showed him the images of the growing girl as she proceeded from the threshold of the first fresco, in purple gown and carrying an offertory bowl of fruit. Then the priestess, receiving an offering as the demi-god Silenus strained, caped and fat and glittering, lyre in hand, at the far edge of the fresco.

Jack laughed and pointed at the grotesque musician,

flapping his lips with farting sounds.

Then back to the initiate, the girl whirling her purple gown in astonishment, then to Silenus again, this time drunkenly holding up the mirror of a silver bowl to an astonished young satyr, and finally, his head missing where the pigment had fragmented and crumbled, the bronze god recumbent in the arms of his mother.

Maddaw, the child whispered. *Jack n Maddaw.*

Madeline held him more tightly, aware now that she would have to give him up.

Quickly she guided him through the last images: the girl emerging from the split cavernous darkness, carrying a staff, then lashed and face down in her nurse's lap, suffering the scourging that led to her being handed the thyrsus, to being prepared for her wedding while Eros held her mirror, this time the silver bowl flattened and smoothed into a flawless reflected glass, wherein she sees herself perfectly for the first and final time.

The two of them—Jack and his Maddaw—fell silent in contemplating such a scene. Though not a religious woman, though frankly not even spiritual, Madeline clung tightly, as I said, trying desperately and at the last moment to shape him into someone who would meet the respectable and predatory standards of her children.

But the whole house knew. By the next day she knew.

And Roy Rausch, in concern for the strangeness of this changeling child, enrolled Jack in the Antioch Baptist School, where the Reverend Peter Koenig could begin to wed this initiate to the good believer's life.

14. Episode: Isaac Clarke

Polymnia: Stephen's past warns him in other, milder ways. Especially as he and George Castille begin to map the production of *The Bacchae.*

Stephen had first seen the play in Ohio. Not a university play, but an alternate guerrilla theatre, its producer, director, and financier a classmate of his named Isaac Clarke—now a family man and music director in an Episcopal church outside of Akron, but then a bisexual Satanist/organist in another Episcopal church, a boy who wrote bad Rimbaud prose poems and intimidated Stephen by being richer, smarter, and certainly more talented than he could dream.

Isaac had gotten on the outside of bad mescaline in his second semester at Kent, and gone home to some wealthy suburb of Cleveland, back into a family of bankers who spoiled and did not understand him.

He returned that spring in a flurry of leaflets. All across the campus the same yellow flyers appeared, stuffed in student mailboxes or stapled to telephone poles, bulletin boards, and almost any wooden surface that would abide them. "Isaac Clarke Presents" took top billing over both *Bacchae* and Euripides. The girl Stephen was dating at the time—a sly classical studies major from New Jersey—found Clarke's sheer hubris enough to make her want to attend.

Stephen milked the connection to impress her, exaggerated his acquaintance with Isaac Clarke in hopes that it would strengthen his acquaintance with the girl. And he succeeded, drawing smiles, a flirtatious touch on his arm, the brush of her lips against his ear as she whispered something about this being Euripides' final play, and so on until the curtain rose on Isaac Clarke facing away from the audience, clad in only a golden lamé jockey strap.

The story, which Stephen did not know, was this: Clarke had cast the play with a number of his smoking companions. Most prominent was his boyfriend of the moment—a young hustler out of Cleveland—as a rather addled Pentheus, who would probably have forgotten the lines even without the hashish. So cast, the play unfolded like a plague spreading, each scene sprawling over the hoots of the audience.

You could almost see Isaac Clarke lose control of the proceedings. By the first scene where Dionysos and Pentheus meet on the stage, cues had been dropped, Tireisias had upstaged Cadmus in a tangle of old men, and the chorus had danced an ungainly ballet that was cut short when a pair of drunken girls in the front row tossed a half-full bottle of Boone's Farm into the maenads' hymn to the ecstatic life with the god. All of this as the audience—college and high school students, young townies, hippies from Cleveland and the gods knew where—talked back to the actors as though they were egging it all on.

It reached its climax when, in their first mutual scene, Pentheus forgot his lines, standing in a kind of hempen stupor. *Well, stranger,* he began, *I believe that women might find you comely, and no doubt that is why you've come to Thebes.*

That to a whoop from somewhere near the back of the theatre, and a surge of laughter that overwhelmed the dialogue.

And then the sound collapsed into a baffled silence, in which everyone seated could hear Dionysos feeding Pentheus lines.

You must never have been a wrestler with that flowing hair… And Pentheus repeating it to the rising derision of the drunken girls, of the townies, of the hooters in the back row, the wronged play staggering toward the horrific final scenes in which the god's followers tear Pentheus apart and bring his body back to Thebes in a blind ecstasy.

But of course by that time, the play itself was wounded. When Agave laments the death of her son, allowing that *it was Dionysos who ruined us*, someone—perhaps the same heckler who had ignited the evening's long ridicule—shouted out, *Well, you done a pretty good job of ruinin' him as well!*

After the play, as the couple walked back to campus, Stephen began to apologize for having brought her into Isaac Clarke's folly. But this much he remembered: as he began to speak, she shook her head, silenced him with a lifted finger, and explained that no, really, it was quite all right.

That in ways it was the god descending.

Though he saw her again on occasion, they never dated anymore, and he once joked to George Castille that he was the first man in the modern age to have a romance undermined by a Greek god.

Oh, honey, George had replied, rolling his eyes. *Perhaps by a Greek god, but not by a goddamned Greek.*

Now, with the first company auditioned, chosen, and assembled, Stephen wonders if he, too, is about to ruin Dionysos. George has already tried to wrest the play from him, conducting reconnaissance among the theatre students at the community college and the high school, weeding out (he claimed) the would-bes and the otherwise untrustworthy, complaining all the while that *The Bacchae* was not a play for this town at this time.

Stephen wonders, as he sits bored through the initial

auditions, whether it was a play that could ever be staged again.

Erato *(calling from the shadows)* **:** My question exactly. If you recall.

Polymnia: Duly noted. Something about a novel, right?

As though she is an expert in genres.

I was speaking of Stephen. Who has cast almost to George's bidding: the De Chevre twins, who (according to George) are the best of the community college actors, will play Agave and Pentheus, Maia mothering her golden-haired brother. Aron Starr, stocky, a little sullen, and high-maintenance like his mother, will play the god.

The first read-through presents problems at once. None of the principals are cooperative: Maia balks at playing her brother's mother, Vincent feels that he should play Dionysos, and Aron is leery that the read is taking place in the apartment of the mildly disreputable Castille.

The reading is drab and cautious, though Stephen has picked a simple translation of the play. Maia and Vincent both sulk, and most alarmingly, Aron is anything but godlike. In fact, Stephen quickly comes to believe that Vincent is right, that the boys should switch roles—Aron the doomed prince, and Vincent the capricious god.

But Aron seems sold on divinity. He will probably quit the production if the swap takes place, and again, after many years, force Stephen to deal with Dolores.

After a long and non-productive two hours, the director drops his copy of the play on the table, gazes dolefully at George Castille, and schedules the next reading for Friday.

"Can't do it," Vincent says. "We all have plans, Mr. Thorne."

And again Stephen hears Jack Rausch's name, this time with more substance. For the boy has invited his new friends to the theatre at the Antioch Church, asking them to critique and coach his performance as George Gibbs in a particularly Baptist production of *Our Town*.

15. Stasimon: Strophe: Polymnia and the Muses

Clio: Now, in the aftermath of meetings, the park seems animate, beyond vegetative. The stage—nothing more than drywall—bristles with moonlight and borrowed life. At the foot of the ruins, water pools and bubbles, life refocillant from the sodden ground, bursting through the boards of the stage.

The whole park is coiling. Sometimes there are convergences, conspiracies of eyes, so that the unseen, which is always implicit, always suing for light and evidence, burgeons into a consent of gazes. The backstage waters bunch and take on substance and scales, the dark eddies at the heart of it condensing to black, glittering points and scanning the slopes of the theatre as the python unwraps and stretches in astonished moonlight.

We watch it happen. The god taking first form in a spring night, in the charged Elaphebolion. So consuming this first transformation that human eyes cannot look on it.

Out of the veil of cannabis we had warned Stephen, *do not look upon it, mortal,* and T. Tommy, caught between stages of being, knew by instinct to turn away. So now we alone watch the water pulse and take on solidity.

Polymnia: There is no god out there. Nor is there anything but the god.

The same mind-body problem the philosophers have tried to get hold of since Heraclitus. The radical wind that fills the park—that lifts the song of T. Tommy's entourage onto Fourth Street—is hot and circuitous.

It rolls all the way south past Stephen's apartment, where he sits at his table now, whiskied and contemplative.

And north it rolls to Oak Street and the intersection the locals call Fourth and Fellini, where crackheads and whores look up, expecting something in the sky, some thunder or rumble of a delivery jet above them.

They see nothing for the street lamps, which are there to help them see, of course.

In the back yard of a brownstone, an incongruous rooster crows, as though the breath of the god brings sun into the artificial day.

The nonexistent god speaks as a blind surge in our blood, as the impulse to live and engender life, to wrestle for power in an unraveling world. But we never meet face to face, never get from the outside to the inside. We dive toward the dark diastole and come up with images and names, like a man who goes round a mirrored stage, looking in vain for a place to stand, seeing only himself on the boards, looking back.

But to see through into the heart of the god, as you yearn to see? Art and religion conspire to keep it from you, the streetlamps that mask your stare into the hollow of heaven. Because it is not pretty there—not your dream of self-actualization nor communion with something that thinks and behaves like you. Ask Moses, whose God passed by him in a dangerous light. Ask

Ramprasad, transformed and glowing with the vision of Kali. Ask Apuleius on his knees before Mother Isis, those witnessing the explosive end of the Gotterdammerüng. Or Jagger at Altamount. Or Spielberg's cinematic Nazis when they open the Ark.

But ask Semele first. Always ask the mother of the god.

Clio: Youngest and most beautiful of Cadmos' daughters, Semele drew the eye of Zeus, because beauty draws all energies in its gaps and caesuras. You know it is breakable because your heart moves toward it, and your heart moves toward it because it is breakable. If Zeus is a metaphor, nonexistent but implicit in the space between things, surely that is part of the meaning when he courts a beautiful mortal: that he stands for our yearning that what we see can last, but he stands at the same time for our knowledge that such things are frangible.

Our desire to worship them goes hand in hand with our desire to break them.

When Zeus's wife Hera found that again he had impregnated a mortal girl, again she plotted harsh revenge. And unable to wreak vengeance on a god, she rose from her throne and headed earthward, wrapping herself in a bright golden cloud and visiting the home of the girl. There she disguised herself as Beroe, Semele's nurse, taking image and form from mortal yearning, from thoughts shaping white hair and wrinkled skin on the forehead of the goddess. Shaping kindness as well, because mortals baffle divinity in trust. You fashion its contours to bank its fire, render it by words you hope you understand.

Melpomene: Semele, then, deceived by simple theatre, spoke to Hera of Zeus. Confused the performer with the character, *actant* with *acteur*. Perhaps something in her confusion jackknifed into the gene pool, because the god her son thrives on misprision such as this.

And in response, the goddess plays at nursemaid, at vague maternal impulse. 'I hope you are right, my dear,' she says. 'But these things frighten me. To *be* Zeus is not enough; he ought to

63

prove his love, if Zeus he is, in all his power and glory, in the form he takes when heavenly Hera welcomes him.

'But, Mother, so he does,' says the girl. 'For those nights in which his seed spills between my thighs are his testimony, his love's proof.'

And 'well, then,' Hera says, her rage now simmering behind a mask benign and sympathetic. 'Well, then, my dear. But surely you know that men often claim to be gods as a way into our beds. But the gods need no rhetoric, no coax and cajole as they ride the deep and recondite currents of dark energy. So beg him, my dear, to reveal himself: to assume his godhead as you raise your knees to his mastery.'

So the goddess shaped Semele's mind, and the girl, in trust that the world was shaped as well by generosity and justice, asked a favor of Zeus as they lay that night in the secret, expectant bed. A favor, any favor, she pleaded, and 'Choose what you will' the god replied. 'I swear by the Power of the rushing River Styx, an oath all gods hold in awe.'

Successful beyond her dreams, happy in her ruin, doomed by charity, Semele answered, 'Give me yourself in the same glory as when your Hera holds you in love's embrace.'

He saw it coming too late. He had sworn his oath, allowed the girl her folly, and her words were out, her wish could never be unwished, his vow never unvowed. In bitterest grief Zeus soared into the sky, trailed by storm clouds and gathering to him lightning and thunder and the bolts that never miss. Even so, he tried to curb his might, and would not wield the fire that steers all things, that kindles and extinguishes, but a lesser fire, forged by the Cyclops and called his second armament. With this in hand he went to Semele in Cadmus' palace. Then her mortal frame could not endure the tumult of the heavens; that gift of love consumed her.

Clio: From her ignited womb the god snatched her baby, still not fully formed, and sewed the child into his thigh, where the young god coiled, foetal and terrible, completing the long gestation. Ino, his mother's sister, in secret from the cradle nursed the child and brought him up, and then the Nymphae of Nysa were given his charge and kept him hidden away within their caves, and nourished him on milk. Down on earth, these things came to place, and Dionysos, baby twice born, was cradled safe and sound.

Polymnia: Though some believe there was another, earlier Dionysos. Zeus his father as well, but the mother Persephonê, that Queen of the Dead snatched by Hades from a sunny hillside. So the dark current draws innocent creatures into the world of the gods.

This Dionysos was Sabazius, or Zagreus. They sacrificed to him at night and in secret, because of the shamefulness of the way Zeus approached his own brother's bride in the shadows, approaching her as a python or dragon, sliding into the tunnels, adits and bolgias of Hades' kingdom, his great coils pulsing with desire and shadow. Past the guardian creatures he moved, lulling to sleep the three-headed dog and Hydra, Briareus, and the triple Chimera.

He crawled to the girl's bedside, his draconic tongue licked her breasts, her stomach, her warm compliant skin, as her womb swelled with his fecund, godly intentions, and she bore Zagreus the horned baby, heir to the throne of the gods, a child with a brow regal and fulgurant.

But Zagreus did not hold the throne of Zeus for long. Some say it was Hera who egged on the Titans, the defeated and forgotten gods; others say that it was their own darkest impulse—jealousy and resentment and malice simple and deep— that brought them from the recesses of the hells where they lay hidden. They daubed their faces with chalk, found the child rapt in front of a mirror, trying to determine just what he was in this world and underworld. They lured him forth with jointed dolls, bullroarers, tops, and knucklebones, those forerunners of dice. By the enticement of toys they drew him out and destroyed him, rent him apart, and spitting him over a fire, began to roast him ceremoniously.

But the death of a god is inconceivable. They rise from the current, the gods, take shape out of dissolution, condense from steam above the dark surge of ichor and blood. So in this story, one among many, the goddess Athena swooped into the flame-haunted shadow in the form of an owl, snatching the child's heart from sacrifice, and bearing it up into the light into the hands of the father.

Here the story branches and joins with other stories, like an alluvial fan of urban legends. Here Zeus makes a potion of the heart, which Semele drinks before his fire and glory overwhelm her. Or here Zagreus rises from ash as the new Dionysos, caped and young like his father, heavy-kneed and pouring rain like his grandpa. Now a lion, now an unbroken horse, now a horned serpent and a tiger and at last a bull, charging the Titans, scattering the gibbering old and ancestral forms of the godflow. It was in this last form, some say, that the god stumbled, and his assailants fell on him with knives. But this time a vengeful Zeus, no doubt his dragon form shed like snakeskin, turned the mirror onto the ancient offenders, trapping them in its reflection, consigning them to the mirrors facing mirrors, images extending into infinitude, to a place in which they saw themselves and themselves only.

Because that is the only hell for those immortal in the first place.

So the Dionysos who was born of Semele in more recent times, whether poured from the heart of Zagreus or burned in Zeus's divine fire and sewn into his thigh to complete the nine-month nightsea journey of gestation....so this Dionysos was feminine, almost delicate, more beautiful than other men. His looks bewitched both male and female, and in turn he was bewitched by them. He would grow into an even more beautiful man, addicted to delights of love. He danced at the head of multitudes, women armed with thyrsus-shaped lances—long-shafted, with the oval heads of pine cones, as if the symbols were not evident already.

So the story in which we find ourselves—my sisters and I. For when all is said and done, aren't the Muses simply maenads on good behavior? Our father was Zeus as well, our mother Memory, and by our songs and dancing, our plays and stories and histories and geometry of heavens, we delight the heart of the god. We school him in mysteries, and become initiates in the *thiasos* of his progress as he moves from one branch of the story to another. It is like a season of tragedies: the cast varies more than the actors. Pan and Silenus dwell with him sometimes as guardians, and again and again he grows up like a creature in some eclogue, now meditative and now lively, the judge and the patron or thymelic song: the verses in honor of the godhead, the processional, the sacrifice.

This is the god I have grown to love. I still imagine myself with the child, instructing him in hymnody, in beautiful devotional verses to cruel and lovely indifference.

I imagine rather than remember. For a daughter of memory I recall actually little. There was a wakening in the dark coffin of a crate bound for somewhere I could not figure, and again in this room under glass and bald light. All of the rest comes to us imagined, conjured from the pulse in the veins of marble at my neck and ear, from the presence of my sisters on the frieze and from the slow intaglio of dreaming.

And yet another story. That the god was entrusted to Hermes, messenger of the gods, who took him to the child's aunt and uncle, to Ino and Athamas, persuading them to bring him up as a girl, to keep the knowledge of him below the sights of the vengeful Hera. But still in pursuit of her rival's son, the goddess drove the couple mad. Athamas, mistaking his older son Learkhos for a deer, stalked and killed and gutted the boy. While Ino threw little Melikertes into a basin of boiling water, and then, carrying both the basin and the corpse of the boy, jumped to the bottom of the sea. Now they rise to help sailors beset by storms: they surface, broken and water-beguiled, from deep and indifferent tides.

16. Episode: Polymnia

Polymnia: He takes the bus, like he is nobody special.

It is a long and tiresome trek from the southeast part of the county, north to where Bardstown Road winds over side streets increasing urban, the houses frame and Victorian brick, the infrastructure crumbling under the dry and potholed pavement.

Jack feels the shudder and heave of the city bus. Feels the gaze of the man two seats behind him, settling on him at a temperature more heated than regard.

He sighs, used to such attentions.

While living with Maddaw and his tutelary aunts, Jack had picked up early that the women's suitors sometimes became his as well. Wealthy and powerful men of all ages would bring him toys and comic books, and by the time he had reached the age of elven or twelve, the comic books had become darker, more lurid, meticulously chosen from back shelves, and instead of toys, he was invited to secluded rooms in Maddaw's sprawling house.

Invited, though he did not follow.

On two occasions, the men (both of them young and seeking political favor from the Rausches), were made nervous in the aftermath of the boy's polite refusal, and panicked at the prospect that Jack would reveal their intentions. They began to pass around rumors that the child had enticed them, that you should watch that boy because he was trouble.

How Jack knew about the controversy was beyond him now: perhaps he had overheard a conversation, perhaps seen one of Maddaw's frequent notes to the Rausch girls, left as guidance on the breakfast table. But the two men were sent packing quickly. One of them, it turned out, had spent his youth as an itinerant companion to older men, one of whom had been killed by a mother in a nursing home firearm accident. The other, a teacher's aide named Silas Wooters, had grown up under the religious guidance of his older brother, a wannabe minister and political hopeful in the city. Neither of them had the social credibility to pass Maddaw's muster, and their accusations were dismissed as madness, both of them banished to towns downstate with accompanying threats.

After the second near-scandal, Jack slipped comfortably into the daily enforced serenity of the local Christian school. He wore his uniform, sat dutifully in class, then came home to read more substantial things and mine the internet for knowledge. He wandered the river banks and played bass in a middle-school garage band. Music liberated him from the confinement of Bible and good behavior: setting the drive and the strong, subterranean flow to the music was, as he saw it, the lot of the bassist, and he listened to the best of his time—Ida Nielsen, Mike Dirnt, D'Arcy Wretsky—then moved back through history to Tina Weymouth, to the omnipresent thump of the funk bands, to Bill Wyman. For one long summer in his fourteenth year, he imagined the music as his ticket out.

But then the suitors returned.

Jack got a glimpse of the Wooters boy at the opening of the Riverfront Amphitheater. Immediately unnerved, he slipped away through the crowd, always looking behind him, back to his school friends and the van ride home. In the back seat the rage overtook him: silent and red the boy fumed between cheery classmates, deflecting solicitous *what's wrong?*s and yearning for the front door of Maddaw's for the house and for concealment. He wasn't going to suffer this, he told himself that night in his room. The suitors had grown to stalkers in the rich soil of his imagination, and the next time one came to call, he decided, he would be prepared for the encounter.

Sure enough, the older man, an exotic sort named Lucius Sora, had come back to the city when Jack was about fifteen. At first there were notes in the water bottle rack on his bicycle. The phone calls began, more frequent in the hours when the caller was sure neither Maddaw nor the aunts were home. Jack didn't see Sora until a week or so after he knew the man had returned, but first sight was disturbing—standing on the opposite side of the creek that flowed next to Maddaw's back property, waist-high in reeds and vines, staring up at Jack's window, looking desolate and beguiled.

The next Sunday afternoon, with the Rausch women off to Louisville for a matinee opera performance of *L'elisir d'amore*, Sora returned to the same desperate spot, this time with a guitar in hand. Waking up late, still in his tighty whities, his window open to draw out the smoke from pirated reefer and tobacco, Jack could hear the song and accompaniment over the soft autumn truckle of the creek.

He looked out over the short stretch of lawn, to the creek and the undergrowth on the other side. Sora, too, was bare to the waist, his voice rising in volume and plaintiveness—singing something about *Be My Baby*, the power of which Jack would understand only later, when he heard the surging, electro/choral version that Tommy and the Brischords laid down when Vincent De Chevre set their *a cappella* to instrument.

The song dripped romance, but when he stepped back from the window, Jack felt its intrusion, its disturbance:

Oh, since the day I saw you
I have been waiting for you
You know I will adore you 'til eternity

He plugged in his bass, moved back to the window, and staring serenely, impassively at the serenade, set down a bass line for Sora's singing. It was more challenge than accompaniment: he didn't know why he did it, what had come over him, but here he was in his underwear on a slanted October afternoon, playing a duet with a would-be seducer, playing seducer in his own right, though he had no interest in Lucius Sora.

No interest beyond a kind of cruel curiosity, and he watched, fascinated, as the vines grew out of the weeds, as they branched and snaked over Sora's chest, gathering thickness and power until they began to tug his arms down, his playing stopped, and the shouts turned quickly into terrified screams.

Oh, Sora had survived, all right. They'd found him near the river bank, his chest and arms cut and reddened with what seemed to be rope burns. He told a story of having ventured up the hill to the Rausch compound, how he wasn't sure what had happened after that, but that the boy up there was trouble and should be watched.

It was where the rumors about Jack had renewed.

Though he had not been inclined toward men— no doubt his great good fortune given the rigidly conservative (and professedly religious) climate in which he came of age—girls, on the other hand, became an early weakness: seduced at thirteen by his Aunt Grace's friend, a realtor who was at least twice his age, popular ever since among girls his age and women decades his senior, Jack had almost unconsciously exploited his physical attractiveness for favors, preferences at school, forgiveness for chronic absences, even the use of classmates' and teachers' cars once he had come of driving age (and actually before that: he was driving the county and state roads in borrowed vehicles at fourteen, fifteen, though he was still a bit cautious about the interstates).

But now, at eighteen he's been bus-bound for about two years, ever since Roy Rausch caught him hotwiring the family Volvo for a trip into the city. Now it is public transit, which gives him time for reverie and thought. So this day, as the bus hisses at a stop. Jack disembarks, hands the driver his transfer, his thoughts on the De Chevre girl as the next bus takes him across the river, back to his confinement at the compound.

He knows he can have Maia on a whim. He figures he could have Vincent as well, the way they both are fussing over him. Vincent doesn't interest him beyond musicianship, and as for Maia, Jack isn't convinced he wants a girlfriend, with all the restraints that come with attachments. A whim would be nice, though, especially if it irritates that tedious, self-absorbed Aron Starr.

Oh, they all are passable friends, better company than he has at Antioch. But that is for the time being. Jack tends to lose interest quickly in the kids around him: he doesn't take well to equals.

Jack settles into the seat as the bus merges with the western traffic, headed for the bridge and home. Out the window battered signs and boarded storefronts flank this stretch of highway, and the sun glares through the broad windshield, shadowing the driver in light.

All said, Jack likes his new companions. They will be fun for a while, and most importantly, they are clever enough to provide a swift and disruptive rescue.

Because if Jack Rausch is restless among the De Chevres and their crowd, he is downright weary of everything regarding Antioch.

17. Stasimon: Antistrophe: T. Tommy Briscoe

(Manent POLYMNIA and THE MUSES, moving upstage to the shadows. Enter TOMMY and THE BRISCHORDS, into the light, center stage.)

T. Tommy: Lao Tzu tells us, children, that *the Tao that can be told is not the eternal Tao,* that *the name that can be named is not the eternal name.* And Chuang-tzu, he says that *the Tao is beyond words,* that *the more you talk about it, the farther away from it you get.*

But Wang Chung saith that *the words we use are strong: they make reality.*

That's my story, and I'm stickin' to it.

Up on the court I am a safety net for middle-aged men. When disappointment and failure come, and you rise a last time toward what you can never be—could never of been in the first place—just as you sink for the last time, you can tell yourself…

At least I'm not that glitterin' fat bastard over to the park.

But I make some reality, children, out of the layers and textures of things.

Time to draw the snake forth from backstage.

It is the way I am gifted. Why I awaken in the hour right before sunrise, while y'all sleep it off and dream of the god. Why you are the entourage and I am the luminary, instead of the other way around.

You learn your gifts of a summer morning. As I did in 1981, on a Southern Parkway easement, two miles from the old city.

It was signified on the overpass that day in August.

I had forgotten the anniversary, the sixteenth, the white-trash national holiday. Was headed north toward town, toward where South Third flows into the Parkway, where I had first entered this town back when Eisenhower was President and where there used to be rolled oysters at a place called Bennie's Back Room.

I saw the name ELIVS, spray-painted in black on the concrete like a moving finger had thereon writ. Someone had misspelled the name of the King. It gave me evidence and a license. LIVES and EVILS, when you turned the letters right. It was a source of great wonderment. Who could of known, after all, how three such words could abide together?

Wise men will tell you that the spelling of things is an arbitrary sign, that the name "Presley" might just as well have been "Boone" or "Bennett" or "Briscoe," that "Elvis Aaron" might of, with simply an alphabetical shift, been named "Jesse Garon" like a dead twin, and that it would of made no difference. But there is deep and gregarious magic in naming, children, magic that draws us and embraces us, where we could almost lie in its lovin' arms, and we can't help falling for it. So maybe there would of been no "Love Me Tender" for Jesse Garon, no "Hunka Hunka Burnin' Love," no Doctor Nick to pump him with amphetamines and consolation.

No T. Tommy Briscoe to carry him on.

Naming him otherwise could of made him otherwise. Could have had everything to do with LIVES and EVILS. And how all of us, including the King himself, draw a veil between 'em, so that, for a brief moment, one cannot touch the other.

The gods are not the past, children. Nor are they far away. Nor are they the gods of your believing, no friendly United Way nor self-help deities out there.

But they are something that has nothing to do with you or me.

Can you hear that pipe in the distance, rising up from over to the Cabbage Patch, gliding over the street sounds like a snake coming out of a Hindu basket? That song enticing, all about wine and muted violence.

Maybe it begun like starlight begins, because though your eye believes the light shines right this instant, it left the surface of the star before the earth was made.

Makes me shudder at the prospect of it.

A song all hushed and filled with portents. Like the night Syrine Landon run into the devil on the way home from church. I swear she did, children, and though it was years ago and she's been forgotten because she wasn't pretty and blonde, the outrage still plays through the air this part of town.

Each of THE BRISCHORDS steps forward in turn, each with a version of Syrine Landon's story.

Falcon Holly: I heared that story. I heared the devil chased her till she turn into a tree. That it's that big, spreading mulberry other side of this park. The one near Sixth.

DJ Mel: Girl, naw. Syrine become part of that creek over to the other park where they seen the goat boy. They say she was drowned, but what it was, was liquefaction.

Daddy Chrome: Liquefaction is the fate of rotting things, MelMel. It's what corpses do, not girls. What happened to Syrine, it happened down at Bernheim Forest. She became a bear, they said. Or someone like her.

T. Tommy: Then I expect I must become definitive. I must instruct you in the laws of physics, which permit no transformation into bear or creek or mulberry. Here is what took place, and it took place like this because I knowed her.

I knowed her family.

Syrine Landon was the source of American dreaming. Grew up in hard country, Jesus-haunted, playing by the rules most of all. Lived down Seventh Street. She was sallow and silent five days of the week, housekeeper and caretaker for her younger sisters Amber Jade and Jade Amber. Only on Saturdays and Sundays and Wednesday nights was Syrine allowed to shine, children. And she shone in the Damascene Holiness Church, where the ecstasy carried good folks unto poison and snakes.

There wasn't a snake that touched Syrine Landon, children. It was as though for a place and time they was a vaporous charm about her, a fog of good intentions, and the boys in the shanties and even the boys at church—well, they saw it and esteemed it for what it was. Because Syrine could of lain on her back with her knees up on her chest and she could of given it up to them, could of settled for the life that such behavior would bring her.

But she didn't, for Syrine had dreams of expanses. Refused them boys, her eyes on school and a decent marriage. She went to Jesus with prayers for rescue, spoke in tongues with the Holy Spirit.

Brischords: *ubi electus facienda cantibus et clara bacchantum voce sonabat.*

T. Tommy: She told me about it.   About resistance and self-denial, how a body behaves for the eyes of God rather than for others, rather than answering the promptings of the inner self. Why she refused them boys.

Why she refused me.

So it was that Wednesday night, the day not yet cooled but the snakes restrained and suppressed, back in their cages and the long Pentecostal wail dying off at Damascene, that Syrine started home, through rows of houses or pine and maple, the night close around her and the summer boding. In the humid shadows she loosened her blouse, let the air in over her rapture-glistening skin there in the dark where nobody could see…

But the devil seen her, to hear the church and family tell, and what he said…

Brischords: What he said was…

T. Tommy: We don't know what he said, children, because if we did, this would be an easy tale.

But he rose from the brambles, or from an alley or even an open brownfield, goatish and large, swollen with night and yearning. And what passed between them was as silent and driven as the deafening pulse of blood alone at the edge of dreaming, and she knew enough to run, poor frightened thing, and did not look back though she knew he was following, and the night slowed, and with it, her rush toward the distant lit windows of her shed of a house.

The brambles pulled at her, or something did, her sisters said.   They seen her intermittent in the light, as though she danced with the wind.   She called out to them, her hands splayed against the screen door, then yanked away from the door as she embraced the shadows or dark arms and was lost to sight.   Then back, her dress loosened and tattered by heat, her white breasts scarred.

Amber Jade and Jade Amber cried out, but they was only twelve, what could they do? as the blackness swallowed Syrine

Landon once again, and the silence swallowed what might of been her screams.

Then out of the derelict shadows come the song of the flute, this song, and they said it was owls, the girls did, and they were too afraid to go to her.

But the morning reassured them, because there is this buoyancy in morning. The sunlight reassembles things, children, and mends them, and all things are open and possible. They went out to look for Syrine Landon, passed through a copse or across a desolate parking lot, where they would find scraps of familiar gingham, a stickiness that snapped and splintered underfoot.

So what good was all that denial, children? Whether it happened a century past or a dozen years ago, it still slips away from understanding—this holding back, this refusal to embrace while you can embrace before the night comes. And the legend has it that, as a form of remorse, the devil made an owl-flute of her finger bones, seven pipes or nine, depending on who tells the legend. And when it plays, you hear it or don't hear it before you are compelled to follow: whether it's inside you or outside you, I'm not the one to say.

I do not remember the color of her eyes, nor do I know whether that Wednesday night ended with her consent or tortured resistance. Nor can I tell you when this happened, nor how the girl's voice sounded in the church or the glade or the side street.

I do know, however, the sound of the owl, and that its rise and falling away is a mask and a deception. For the song has not ceased since that Wednesday, and it will continue, dark or day. And once it is gone, the night will be quiet at last.

18. Episode: Polymnia

(Exeunt TOMMY and THE BRISCHORDS. POLYMNIA moves center stage.)

Polymnia: Aron sleeps uneasily, his dreams half-borrowed from the films he has seen at the Shangri-La.

The vintage theater has outdone itself this spring. Aron has gone to all the films, each a half-century old and chosen for its "Monsters from Outer Space" theme. The last night had been a double feature: *Earth vs. the Flying Saucers* and *Invasion of the Body Snatchers* ("the good one," Apache Downs had insisted, "not the Donald Sutherland one") had capped off a series that began with *The Thing*, sliding sensationally through *Invaders from Mars* and *War of the Worlds* before ending the list with "an evening of alien terror."

It was the best evening, complete with popcorn, a great view of Maia De Chevre only two seats down from him. She lounged on the other side of her brother, drinking an impossibly large beaker of soda Aron had bought for her with almost the last of his week's money. As they waited for the first film, the boys—all of whom were about half as clever as they thought they were, but twice as clever as Aron—scrambled over one another in their attempts to amuse Maia. Aron gaped at them with admiration, wishing he had the looks and the wits to impress the one girl in the company.

"This Snatcher's better than the remake," Apache had repeated, for what must have been the fifth time. He was fishing for a *why?* that would set him to lecturing.

McCarthy Hearings. Cold War. Commie in a pod in a greenhouse. The usual Wikipedia take on the film.

Aron had heard the interpretation. Was bored with it by now. Hoped to whatever god might be listening that Maia wouldn't be taken in by borrowed brilliance, though he figured he was safe on that front, that Apache's looks would keep him out of contention.

The real rival was miles away, rehearsing *Our Town* at Antioch.

Aron has admired and hated Jack from the moment they met at the game. Jack's serenity and luck, his beauty and humor, lifted him instantly above the others in the group, and Aron rankles at the intrusion, his role as supporting actor confirmed in the new boy's arrival.

At first, Aron believed and dearly hoped that Jack was gay. Boys were not that pretty, not that mild. But scarcely a few minutes from their meeting, when Jack turned his eye toward Maia and the air popped and bristled with their mutual regard, Aron saw trouble on the rise.

It was no accident, then, that his dreams have scuttled down this awful alley.

Aron dreams he is in the neighborhood—the park, the amphitheater, the court to the south and the gnarled, legendary Witches' Tree to his north. He stands among the tiered benches, looking down on the stage. The air is astringent with juniper, sweet with mulberry.

Jack Rausch walks onto the stage, capped and dressed in a white shirt, knee pants, and galluses. He is George Gibb from Our Town, wholesome and filial and gee-whiz, but Aron sits too far from him to be reassured by any irony.

Now Jack begins his transformation, lifting his arms in a torchlight rising from nowhere. A hot wind rising from the mulberries passes over the two of them, ruffling Aron's long and stringy hair, but slowly unraveling Jack's shirt, until he stands bare-chested center stage, his shoulders dappled and scaled with shadow.

Jack returns Aron's gaze, smiling enigmatically, his dark eyes glittering and impassive.

Aron feels the wood of the bench roil and sprout beneath him, and branches and vines rise from its back and encircle his chest, clutching him tightly, contracting, crushing him in a slow, inevitable embrace. He calls to his friend on the stage, but Jack sits down, still smiling, wearing only a loin cloth now, the moon bright and deceptive across his dark torso.

How do you like me now, Aron Starr? the air whispered, and Aron awakens, sweating and gasping, not quite remembering what has passed for dreaming in the imperiled night.

19. Episode: Reconciliations

Polymnia: Hands in pockets, seated in the row above George Castille, Stephen allows it had been a disappointing evening.

They have sent Vincent and Aron to clear away a quartet of vagrants who have been singing by the amphitheater stage, standing in the orchestra. One of them, a shiny fat man, stands ground almost defiantly, but then three others joined the boys—young men Stephen assumes are their classmates—and the band of drifters trails away into the dusk.

Now George Castille lights a cigarette and stares down into the shimmering geometry of the mirrored shards on stage, the smoke crowning his head and coiling in the still air.

"It's odd," George observes, "to see young actors running on technique alone. It's supposed to be geezers like us who go through the motions but this bunch is just reading lines. If you ask me, it's time for early and radical changes. We need a translation that sounds like human language rather than this literary nonsense. We may even need to shuffle the roles around a little."

Stephen reaches over and cadges one of George's cigarettes. "Shuffle the roles?"

George nods. "Regard, if thou wilt, young Vincent. Gorgeous and sporting a golden spiral of hair. You know he looks more godlike, Stephen. Maybe Aron is better as Pentheus, after all. And honestly, before you spend too much time and energy in production, you might even consider another play. *Antigone* is easier to follow. It's *Sophocles*, for god's sake, and makes some sense. And there are a million translations. They read it in high school all the time, so the language has to be on a fourth-grade reading level. Which works for around here, you know."

Stephen shakes his head. "*Antigone* has a huge cast."

"That's an excuse, Stephen. You can double roles, and you know I can get you the walk-ons from the college. Those kids are itching to pad a resume."

Stephen takes a deep drag from the cigarette. "Excuse or no, I'm standing ground on *The Bacchae* and on this translation."

George shrugs. "But how about the casting, dear?"

"Well. If you can get Aron and Vincent to switch roles, I'm all behind it. Vincent certainly is more handsome and...and poised than Aron. But for some reason, Aron is clinging to the god role."

"Oh, he wants to be a *star*. Don't we all?"

"No, George. This is enthusiasm. Sometimes enthusiasm is enough."

George nods. "The Greeks called it *entheus*, how the god spoke through the actor. The tragic mask is a symbol of that. The god occupying receptive shape, seeing through its eyes and breathing and speaking through its mouth. An actor—even a young one like Aron or Vincent—has moments in which the words usher forth Dionysos, or Apollo, or whatever god is present."

Stephen laughs. "No professorial lectures, old friend. Especially those that miss the mark like a bad arrow. Because the words themselves are masks. Lest you forget it, words are not the voice of the god any more than the mask is his face. The actor and director bring them to life. No conjury in words, as far as I can tell.

"Now, the stage, on the other hand, has some possibilities. Especially *this* stage. We might be lucky that the mirrors from your old *Hamlet* are still up. Those that haven't been broken and scattered. We could use them to confront the audience, to let them see the side of things that stage illusion usually hides. How might it work if you could sit in the crowd and see, by reflection, an actor remove one mask and put on another?"

George shook his head. "Why on earth would you want to do that?"

"I want masks, George. Like the original."

"And lose the advantage that Vincent is prettier than Aron?"

"We could still see them both behind the masks, if only for a moment as the boys put them on. The audience would remember the difference in beauty as the scene unfolds. Like the beauty of their souls in comparison."

George shakes his head. "Does a god even *have* a soul, Stephen?"

A call from the court interrupts them. The streetlamps were just coming on, and Maia approaches them, a taller woman walking beside her.

It takes Stephen a moment to recognize Dolores Starr. "Oh, not her!" he mutters.

George rolls his eyes. "Don't borrow trouble, Stephen. You think there'll be a confrontation because you can't imagine a part of the world that has nothing much to do with you. You've imagined this grudge for ages, rehearsed it in your mind until you've cast her as some kind of Medea. Was she that bad when you saw her at the high school? She's just checking on her son."

Maia approaches, and with a sweet, perfunctory greeting, leaves them to join the young people milling on the shadowy stage. Dolores sits on the bench beside George, and holds out her hand. George drops a pack of Winstons into it, and she lights one, French-rolling the smoke from mouth to nose in an ecstasy of nicotine.

"I understand," she exhales, "that my son is to be the god of the vine."

George and Stephen exchange glances. Stephen catches the whiff of wine in the smoke, smells it on Dolores' skin.

"We read through the play this afternoon, dear," George replies at last.

Dolores smiles. "Good. Very good. Oh, George, do you remember the trouble with arranging those mirrors?"

George nods. "Oh, Stephen, the *task* of it all. We wanted the set to seem like it revealed backstage, like you were saying before. But only the backstage we *wanted* to reveal."

"The illusion of transparency," Stephen says, feeling the needle.

"Or the transparency of illusion, either way. At any rate, Dolores and I spent hours tilting each mirror so it caught only so much reflection from the others. For a while we entertained the idea, Stephen, of positioning me between two mirrors that directly faced each other, so that there would be Hamlets regressing boundlessly. And of course I would stand between them when I said, *I could be bounded in a nutshell, and count myself a king of infinite space, were it not that I have bad dreams.*

"Clever," Stephen remarks vaguely.

George stirs the smoky air with a wave of his hand. "Oh, far from it, I know. Just too obvious, like that production of Coriolanus where we thought about making him a motorcycle gang leader. It could have worked, after all…"

"Just not so…"

George snorts. "*Avant.* Just not so *avant*, Stephen. Not that it made any difference to that hideous old queen Wade Abner."

Dolores and Stephen share their first conspiratorial glance in about two decades. The feud between Castille and Abner is long-standing and nails-out.

"I remember, George," Stephen soothes, hoping the old conflict won't erupt into another of Castille's haranguing soliloquys. "If it's any consolation, Abner's still the drama critic for the paper only because he has a knack of knowing whose bottom to kiss. How else would you survive two changes of ownership and a corporate takeover?"

"Well, my bottom was never kissable, apparently," George grumbles. "What was it he said? *Histrionic, from its arm-waving Danish Prince down to the funhouse mirrors in which he seemed to have lost himself and his dignity?*"

Dolores and Stephen laugh, as some strange coldness breaks against the reconfigured air. "I'm sorry, George," Dolores says at last. "But it *is* rather a funny line."

"It is an insult," George says, lifting his chin and squaring his shoulders, "from which I am still recovering. The old virago is right about one thing, though: somehow I lost the way and ended up in musical comedies."

Now the three of them sit silent, watching the young people roughhouse and dance across the disheveled stage.

Somewhere at the edge of the park, near the bus stop by Fourth and Fellini, a chorus of voices is singing "Love Me Tender."

Then they see Jack Rausch approach and climb the stage gracefully. There was no way not to be bewitched. They stand, watch for a breath-catching moment, then part, Stephen down toward the stage, George on foot toward the Court, and Dolores to her car, bound for wherever she heads this time of cool and humid night.

20. Episode: Bathophobia

Polymnia: On center stage, five boys sit Indian-style, like points of a star.

Billy and Apache pass a cigarette back and forth like a doob. Vincent and Aron huddle with Jack Rausch.

Aron is going on about the *Hamlet* of George Castille.

Hamlet couldn't make up his mind, Aron insists. That is his problem. It is what they say at the beginning of Olivier's *Hamlet*, after all. And we all know that is the best version.

Vincent nods absently, his eyes settling and fixing on Jack Rausch, accepting the half-smoked cigarette from Billy Shepard. The smoldering glow of the tobacco lights the newcomer's dusky skin, the dark eyes with a hint of his mother's epicanthic fold. The other boys' heads turn toward him, seeking news from a faraway country.

"My mother designed these sets," Aron says. "Feel like I'm in a fuckin funhouse."

"Wasn't that what the reviewer said, Aron?" Vincent

mutters. All the boys except Jack Rausch laugh wickedly.

"The reviewer said 'fuck'?" Billy Shepard asked, which sets them all laughing again. The laughter fades as Stephen approaches.

"Next Tuesday," Stephen says, "we'll read again," You can see him take in the faces of the unfamiliar boys, nodding *howdies* to the new ones, his gaze finally settling on Jack Rausch.

Later, the boys stand in front of Dolores' Starr's array of mirrors. Each one can see himself and himself and himself, diminishing to a vanishing point. But as each boy stands there and looks, the others see nothing. The mirrors are inverted, turned on each other and to the interiors of the viewer.

But time and a rainy fall, vagrants and crackheads and a hard freeze in November has dislodged some of the glass. Now the upstage center mirror—the one Dolores Starr had designed to show the back of Hamlet, or rather of George Castille—had fallen on its side. Now, as if by accident, it faced the mirror upstage right.

And it is between these glasses that Aron Starr and Jack Rausch find themselves, alone and together for the first time.

"'Sup," one says, more statement and challenge than question.

The other looks up, and they recognize each other in the smeared image.

Jack sees something familiar and startled and furtive about Aron. Meets his gaze until Aron lowers his eyes finally— something Jack encounters wherever he goes, and takes as the way to greet and be greeted. He watches the pulse of blood at Aron's throat, hears the pounding of the jugular.

Aron sees Jack as familiar and larger, more indistinct, as though the glass ripples across his features, blurring and obscuring them. For a moment the face seems to gather definition, as Jack widens his eyes and meets Aron's gaze. Aron will dismiss it later, will set aside the thought that Jack's pupils expanded until they engulfed the iris, then the scleras, until Aron looked away, baffled by the strange swimmer's terror of riding a current over a shadowy underwater crevasse.

Bathophobia. Aron has looked it up. Has endured the taunts of Apache and Billy, who claim it meant fear of bathing.

So now he moves the conversation to safer, shallow waters, and speaks to Jack of mirrors and reflections, sparring with words. How you can't see the vampire in a mirror, though you could in *Nosferatu*, in Anne Rice, and in the horrible new glittering incarnations of *Twilight* for which he expresses hot hatred while Jack claims a serene indifference.

But the mirrors, Aron continues. Was it antipathy to silver? transparency? an absence of souls that the mirror could contain?

Then Jack recalls a history of reflected boys, the ones of older stories: Hylas and Hermaphroditos tugged under by nymphs as they admired themselves in still waters, and Narcissus pining away in love of the likeness that met his eyes. Aron knows the stories, is surprised at how immediate they seem. It is as though Jack evokes them through whisper and reflections, brings them to life until Aron is uncertain whether he is learning the tales, discovering or remembering them, or somehow making them up himself.

They stand before the mirror young and beautiful, susceptible to its drowning pools: Jack and Aron looking at Jack and Aron in an infinity of crouching speculation, in all cases Jack's hand placed tentatively on the larger boy's shoulder. For a moment the surface of the glass troubles, and both boys squint to look into supposed distances, catching a glimpse of something glittering down a corridor of corridors, into amphibolous night.

21. Episode: First Reviews

Polymnia: Stephen admits to the boy's perfection as the old men sit in George Castille's apartment.

George Castille refilled the wine glasses. "Beautiful and guileless, yes. And the others *defer* to him. Almost genuflection, did you see it? But the fundies have netted Jack Rausch. Yes, he acts, but in productions of *Our Town* and The *Fantasticks*. And those innumerable bad Christian dramas that Antioch serves up."

Stephen looks over the lip of his glass into the red pool of Lachryma Christi. Breaks the surface tension of the wine with a touch. "He's perfect, nonetheless. And if not an actor, I understand from Vinnie, who should know, that the boy plays a wicked bass. It's *The Bacchae*, damn it, and we need music—original music—for a play about Dionysos. I want some part in the play for Jack Rausch."

It is deep night on the Crescent Hill porch where the two men sit, smoking and drinking and speculating on the future of the play. Already it looks as though long, hard rehearsals might end up with nothing to show but an amateurish performance.

"For God's sake, George," Stephen laments. "I can't even cast the damn thing! You know we'll end up as the two old men, you and I, and Maia is woefully young to play her own mother, which is what she is if we're to believe Vincent is her son. I'm sorry…no amount of makeup… Then there is Aron. He's workmanlike enough, but short on the charisma, like somehow the die is cast against him. You saw him shrink away from the Rausch boy, cede the stage to him, for crying out loud, and I could use that, could hinge the play on it. What wouldn't I give for a production in which my Pentheus is naturally afraid of the invading god? I'd love to have Jack Rausch in this play."

George rolls his eyes and sighs. "You can get a kid to play fear, Stephen. It's called acting, and it's the one emotion they can do. They're close to it because they're afraid of everything. And Jack is afraid as well, I'd wager. The Reverend Peter Koenig has the boy on a short leash over there—Jack's from a prominent family in case you've forgotten—and there's no way the reverend will loosen his grip, especially to let loose the likes of us upon America's impressionable youth."

"I suppose," Stephen concedes. "But here is the thing about Koenig. I know him a little—met him through Dolores, at a time when she wasn't too fond of me."

"Unlike now?"

"I know, I know. But actually the drinking has mellowed her. I met Koenig back when Dolores was still staring poison my way, giving me that narrowed-eye glare that's genetic issue to angry white-trash girls, though Dolores would be appalled to know she's still numbered in that group. I suppose you know she and Koenig dated a little back in the day—a ridiculous match, but Dolores was never good at pickin' them.

"At any rate….Koenig. Met him at a couple of theatre events. He went out of his way to be decent, all the time that Dolores was doing her best Joan Crawford. I asked him why so civil, knowing how Dolores felt, and he went on about peace and reconciliation—things he was supposed to talk about as a minister, I thought at the time, but I ended up rather liking him despite that kind of earnest thing that preachers do. They say he's changed, become sanctimonious enough that they like him at Antioch. But I remember him younger and in character."

"Just a new part, I'm guessing," George says, reaching in his pocket for the now-crumpled pack of Winstons. "Just because he can be the *religieux du jour* doesn't mean they *all* can act at Antioch. Jack Rausch could be the Baptist Keanu, lovely and dreadful."

Stephen laughs. "May I have another of those smokes, George? So what you're saying is that we go to the dance with the cast what brung us?"

A car rushes uphill over the cobbled street below them— one of the few left unpaved in Louisville, a picturesque and suspension-crippling obstacle course of masonry. As always, the sound passes like a remote and remembered thunder.

"I think we should assume that's the way things will be, Stephen. It's the way in our town: we're Jesus-haunted and judgment-drunk, like we've been since the Great Awakening. Nothing's going to change in this town. Unless…"

He looks at Stephen and winks. "Unless, of course, Jack Rausch can be and will be rescued."

22. Episode: The Qeej

(EUTERPE joins POLYMNIA center stage, wearing a laurel crown and carrying a double-reeded aulos. She sits, cross-legged and POLYMNIA's feet, and begins to play accompaniment to the story.)

They sit on the tiered upper platform of the stage. The other boys are busy shifting the mirrors, as Stephen had requested before he left, but Jack sits down by Maia, lying back and peering through the netting of new leaves at the encircling street lamps.

It is time for them to get home. The police precinct headquarters lie at the other side of the grounds, but the residents know that by this time of night the officers had been dispatched south toward the university and north along Fourth Street as it passes by Park, by Ormsby, and to the notorious intersection of Fourth and Oak, better known as *Fourth and Fellini* for the company you keep there.

Maia hugs her knees and half-closes her eyes. Something in Jack Rausch settles her, and when he lies by where she is sitting, steepling his fingers under his head, it's as though she floats at the edge of a light and restful sleep, the traffic noises from Fourth Street fading into the cry of migratory birds, into the whirr and bull-roaring ratchet of newly emerged cicadas, weeks early this year, they say.

She tells Jack she is single—*between boyfriends*, she says.

"But that's pretty recent, isn't it?" he asks, the cicadas suddenly revving down as if to make room for her answer.

"It is. How did you know?"

He smiles and shrugs. "You said *between boyfriends*. That's how. And is it cramped between them?"

She hugs her knees tighter, surprised that she is about to answer this boy, ingenuous and almost two years her junior. But Jack is evocative: there is a space around him that is calmly tidal, where attentions circle and still. So she tells him about the heartbreak of Cowboy Copass.

EUTERPE provides a low, inveigling accompaniment upon the aulos. Fully in the light now, the Muses gather around them.

Polymnia: Nurtured at Maia De Chevre's high school, Billy Copass had received the nickname to rhyme with his grandfather's favorite entertainer. He blossomed early, was the recurring dream of Kentucky's land grant university—6'3 and white, with an arching jump shot they called *Copass's compass*. The coaches in Lexington knew two things at first sight: that Cowboy was good enough only to ride the end of the bench and shoot three-pointers near game's end, but that a white guard always guaranteed state-wide adoration.

Cowboy was the whole package, but saddled with a fourth-grade reading level. That was where Maia had joined the nurturing, guiding him through the maze of class work in his junior and senior years. In return for her kindness, he had deflowered her, made the southern commute to school, and dumped her for a debutante the past October. Maia knew as well as anyone that he would try to reconcile when Lexington left him stranded—social class and horse money would eventually trump athletic celebrity, and Cowboy would sell insurance or run for State Legislature. But that would be later, and he was already as good as gone to her, a strange narcotic dream of high school glory.

Jack seems to understand her story. His almond-shaped dark eyes stir her guilelessly, and she feels awakened by his regard. She tells him about her songs and her poems and her stage dreams suddenly unveiled. In return Jack simply listens, at the end of her accounts showing her his necklace, from which hangs a small copper charm he claims had belonged to his mother. It is a *qeej*, he says, spells it, then pronounces it *gheng* again to her confusion and amusement.

"Vietnamese pipes," he says. "Played most often at funerals, so there's a sadness to them. But the notes make a language, they say. Each note is a word. And there's a legend to its making."

It is Maia De Chevre's turn to listen.

EUTERPE sets down the aulos. THE MUSES bend over her like weeping willows. She speaks softly at first, her voice strengthening in time and assurance.

Euterpe: Jack tells her this: that long ago in Vietnam, there was a hero by the name of Sinsay. Sinsay was a great and eager warrior, and after each victory, he would marry one beautiful woman from the kingdom he conquered, enjoy a brief honeymoon, then move on.

Maia thinks this sounds familiar, wants to lament her own lot, but Jack is off on the tale, which slowly becomes not about her, not about him.

Eventually, Jack tells her, Sinsay had conquered seven kingdoms and married seven brides.

One day, the Great King—the liege lord of Sinsay—decided to have a festival. Everyone was invited and excitement was high, especially for the seven young wives Sinsay had left behind in the care of their families. They knew their husband would be there, and each made her own plans to find Sinsay and be reunited with him. Sinsay, too, looked forward to attending the festival, to be praised as a champion and to find his seven wives.

When the fair began, Sinsay searched the crowd for his wives, and each of them searched for him. But it had been so long since they parted that he could not recognize them, nor could they recognize him. Disappointed but unwilling to give up the search, each wife began to sing her own *lug txaj*, courtship songs that only a husband or wife would know.

Jack spells *lug txaj* and pronounces it again for Maia.

By following their *lug txaj*, Sinsay finds each of his wives. And, one by one, he sang *lug txaj* back to the women, acknowledging each to be his wife.

But the women were angry to find that Sinsay had seven wives. They quarreled over him until the Great King finally intervened, posing them a task. If all seven were wives, he said, each will be able to make something that can speak her *lug txaj*. If not, her claim was not true.

So the wives went home, and in nine days each came back with a pipe. At first, each pipe made only a sound, a note, and both Sinsay and the king were perplexed. But the women smiled, for they knew better. You see, they had learned in the absence and the making. So when the seven pipes were put together into one instrument, Sinsay blew through the reeds, and it made words. So the great king declared that all of the women were Sinsay's true wives.

Maia is not sure she likes the story. But she leans against Jack's shoulder as he continued, looking out over the stage toward the old park promenade, the stone lions and the row of trees to their west.

According to legend, he tells her, the *qeej* once had powers far beyond making words. The master *qeej* players were wizards who could fly through the air, read other people's minds, disappear, and set enemies on fire. Wizardry was a guarded art, learned only from the master and tested in competitions. At first these contests were just to show how much each player had learned. But over time, they became harsh, ill-natured, and the masters took away the magic part of the teaching until the *qeej* was another flute. Because the masters did not pass on this learning, the magical powers of the *qeej* were lost.

"You almost sound like you believe the story," Maia says, expecting, in this moment of intimacy, Jack will confess he does.

But instead he laughs merrily, and rubbed the copper pendant between his thumb and forefinger. "Oh, not at all, Maia!" he replies, and for a moment, caught in the shadow and artificial light, the *qeej* seems to glow white upon his skin. "I expect we should be going now. Aron's been glaring at us ever since I sat down here."

23. Episode: American Fire

(EUTERPE resumes her soft, doleful melody on the aulos. The other MUSES dissolve into shadow, in a rending of light that scatters soft sparks across the stage. Now EUTERPE is alone with POLYMNIA, who begins to speak.)

Polymnia: They offer him a ride across the river. For a moment Jack accepts, but when he sees Aron's glare of disapproval, he decides the time is not right, not just yet. He declines, telling his new friends there is a cousin nearby whom he wanted to visit.

Which is partially true.

Traveling north over Park Avenue, stepping by the Witches' Tree with only a casual glance into its lower branches, Jack makes for the back door of the Oscar Wilde, a bar near the corner of Fourth and Fellini. A distant cousin from the old country, a middle-aged character named Pham Thanh, tends the bar his partner owns: the two men share a house as well, a block or so down Fourth Street, and Thanh is always available for fatherly advice and an avuncular cot for the night.

As always, like a test of heritage, Jack's cousin addresses him first in Vietnamese, and feigns disappointment when the boy cannot answer. Jack promises himself yet again that someday he would surprise the older man with a fluent reply, but Vietnamese lies just beneath his memory, the sound of it recognizable but not quite intelligible, like the thump of a bass line on the radio of a car or a low growling from a distant copse—briefly making sense and then vanishing, a brief pattern he can recollect from infancy.

The strange nostalgia vanishes when Thanh begins to scold him. *You are late. Almost ten o'clock now, Jack, and you know the crowd change in here, with all the grown men. No, you not come into the bar now. Here is the key to the house. You go there, watch the television. Sleep in the guest room.*

Why you not catch the bus back home?

It is difficult to explain, of course. When Thanh had been Jack's age, he'd been dodging the conflict in Củ Chi Province rather than wading through high school crises. NLF, NVA, USA, had all ben dangerous acronyms that sent him for cover. He hadn't had the time to fret over flirtations, jealousies and betrayals.

Jack, on the other hand, knows the terrain of his own border wars. Aron is fighting him through disguise and masquerade—whether on the stage of the amphitheater on in the role-playing game he seemed to have ruled until Jack stepped in and changed the protocol. It is safer conflict—no weapons beyond wits and intrigue—and Aron is already flustered.

It is a battle Jack will win.

For a minute he meets Pham Thanh's gaze, cousin looking to cousin at the back door of a quiet, domestic gay bar. Jack tries and fails to intuit Thanh's history: though he knows from extended family that his own story is dotted with darkness and tragedy, somehow he cannot find his way to those provinces, to the tunnels, to that bomb-battered country. His story is a step removed from worldly sorrow. Briefly, vaguely, he understands, as he wanders back down Sixth Street to the house his cousin shares with the Wilde's owner, Alan Stack. Understands in a serene, impassive way: Jack searches his emotions for an expanse of heart, for empathy or even sympathy, but he uncovers only a kind of calm curiosity.

It is good, he figures, that Thanh Pham has survived. And being around him is a comfort.

Now Jack passes close to the Witches' Tree—the center of urban legend in the park for at least a few months more—and looks up through its leaves, past the rosaries and dream-catchers, the mala beads and the plastic cherubim, to where the spring moon, full at last, seems tangled in the height of the bifurcating limbs.

People climbed these branches to enlightenment. That's what the kids tell him.

So why not? he asks himself, and sets his foot to a low burl on the trunk of the tree. Hoisting himself to a low branch, he sits and looks down across the park. His vision sails easily through the row of maple and mulberry, crests the top of the amphitheater, and passes over roof and court to an open window in a disheveled brick townhouse on Second Street within speaking distance of the Mag Bar. Were Jack more uncertain, less comfortable with contradiction, he might wonder whether he actually sees Aron Starr standing at the window, or whether he imagines the sight from moonlight and from the witchery of the surrounding amulets.

Aron looms in the window frame, plotting misdemeanor.

Son of a drama teacher, aspiring actor, he has learned to struggle in masquerade, to face down enemies through veils. Now, at barely ten in the evening, he braces for a long night of it, for plots too elaborate, too overthought.

He can almost feel eyes on him as he contemplates murder.

Oh, not a literal, knife-to-the-throat homicide. What is decent in Aron recoils at *that* prospect, though less at the actual deed than at the fear of getting caught in the act. Murder by metaphor is more like it: a slippery, dramatic gesture that cannot be pinned down as a threat but can be felt, deeply and subliminally, as though Jack Rausch calls it from memory rather than meeting it head on. He wants Jack to intuit danger without locating its source, to back away without fixing him in his sights.

His thoughts settling on a first and tentative plan, Aron steps away from the window, feeling suddenly safer in what he mistakes as a confidence of purpose. His bedroom feels suddenly smaller, more enclosed: he supposes it is a kind of protection.

24. Episode: The Game's Revenge

(Upstage rises a thin, backlit curtain. Behind it, five people are seated at a table, visible in silhouette. POLYMNIA steps downstage right.)

Polymnia: Again the flicker of multicolored dice behind the cardboard screen, as Aron plots the late-night game.

The party has descended to the fifth circle of the imaginary maze, and it is Aron's task to plan out the monsters, obstacles, and puzzles they will encounter on their way downward to rescue the enchanted prince.

But now he scrawls notes listlessly on a legal pad, no longer in the mood for gaming.

He had walked to the back of the stage, down the gentle slope behind it, his thoughts still troubled by the distortions in the mirror. He had gone almost to Fourth Street when voices, overheard and unfamiliar, reached him from the bus stop, where he saw four shapes—ragged and gesturing—whose presence made him turn back.

But on the battlements of Hamlet's Elsinore designed by his mother last spring, he saw Jack and Maia, silhouetted by street light, sitting and talking too close to each other. He hoped what he suspected about Jack was true, which would make it simply two pals conniving. Nevertheless, the sight unsettled and annoyed him, even though he was certain by now that he had no chance with Maia.

Now, three nights after the rehearsals and betrayals, he watches her take a seat by Jack. He bristles as the dark boy draws the chair out for her. Nosed down into scrawlings and rulebooks and hexagonal maps, half-heartedly Aron pencils in array of adversaries and a series of traps, descriptive phrases and columns of numbers to be transformed by his storytelling into something fantastical and plausible.

His friends make a rather absurd party to begin with, he decides. All of them play to their weaknesses. Apache's character was a nimble and confident thief, Billy Shepard's a fighter with maximum strength and almost as much agility, while Vincent's is a druid whose light guided the party through subterranean intricacy. And Maia's magic-user is poised and resourceful, has a tactic for every predicament, a spell for every jam. Perhaps their greatest roleplay, Aron decides, is passionately being whatever they are not.

He is the one who knows the rules, who improvises ingeniously, knows when to fudge dice rolls and when to stick to the letter. If he says so himself, he is no shabby game master.

But even in this setting, in the world Aron Starr has created for his friends, Rausch is an intruder, a disruption. All those great preliminary dice rolls ensure he can play virtually any character in this quasi-medieval universe, and he had chosen a cleric, of all roles. A female cleric at that.

Ambrosia, Jack has named his character. Aron guesses it is some kind of inside joke. Sullenly he adds a row of numbers and covers his legal pad with notes to himself.

Meanwhile, Maia and Jack are going on about *Our Town*.

Aron joins in from behind the game master's screen. "How

can you stand it, Jack? Cheesiest play in Western drama, and they give you the cheese of the cheese. George Gibbs, for God's sake. Romantic lead in a play totally without romance."

Jack shrugs and laughs, letting Maia make things worse by rising to his defense.

"Oh, Aron, it isn't *that* bad. Everyone produces it now and then. Mr. Castille makes fun of it, and even *he* produces it sometimes, because it guarantees a packed house. It's gentle and calm in a sad way, and it kind of appeals to everyone, even if they don't admit it."

"It's sentimental," Aron insists. "It's weird, and nothing really happens. If it was a movie you'd walk out on it thirty minutes in."

"What *does* happen?" Apache asks.

Jack clears his throat. "It's mainly the daily lives of an American family. Maybe even *the* American family, you know? First act kinda sets up two families, living next to each other. They have kids—George Gibbs and Emily Webb—who are sweet on each other and eager to grow up. Second act is all about their wedding, and between the second and third act Emily dies in childbirth, so the third act is all about her as a kind of ghost going back in time and seeing the everyday she had as a kid and realizing how important the little things are."

"Pretty lame," Apache says, as Billy and Aron nod in agreement.

"But there's other things besides action and big events, Aron." Jack speaks to Aron alone, ignoring the other boys. "I mean, if George Gibbs stalked the town mutilating and eating everyone like Hannibal Lecter it might have some cool moments, but what's important is almost never what is settled that way."

"I know," Aron snaps, his patience fraying. "War is not the answer, and whatever. Roll for initiative."

Which means that the first game encounter of the evening is ready to begin. *Rolling for initiative* means the start of combat, and Aron has imagined a tight spot for his adventurers: a party of ten orcs whose number he has just increased to fifteen out of spite. He usually lets his characters explore their surroundings for a few minutes, soak the atmosphere he loves to create and describe, but he feels combative tonight.

As always, Apache rolls for the party. This time a four.

Behind the screen Aron rolls a three, but he announces it as a five to the players, and moves first in the streamlined, simple combat of board movement and dice.

From the beginning, the players can tell that the feel of the game has shifted. As the die rolls alternate and the orc casualties pile up, Aron swears under his breath several times at Jack's high tosses—something they'd all laughed about in earlier sessions, but has become (inexplicably to most, if not all of them) a serious matter.

"Three orcs approach Ambrosia, their scimitars drawn," Aron intones.

Jack frowns at the circumstance. "Ambrosia steps back, casts an Inflict Light Wounds spell on the first of 'em. Is that how it's done?"

Aron nods brusquely, masks his roll again. "Roll for damage."

Jack tossed the rhomboid eight-sided die against the game-master's screen. "Seven!" he exclaims, and his fellow players look to the game master with satisfaction—indeed, with a little smugness that Aron certainly notices.

"The orc reels, but keeps coming."

"With seven points' damage, plus 2 for Ambrosia's level?" Billy protests.

Aron peers over the screen. "Five points max for the spell, Billy....I mean, Hrothgar. Check the rules."

Billy reaches for the Game Master's Guide, but Jack waves him away. "He's in charge, Billy. He knows the rules and applies them fairly."

Aron frowns and rolls the dice again. "The second orc brings his scimitar across in a savage slash, its blade descending on the dark locks of Ambrosia. " Then looks up. "It crashes hard into her shoulder, cutting bone and gristle…"

"Aron!" Maia exclaims.

"Six points damage," Aron announces. "The orc has initiative, slashes across again…"

Maia looks to her brother, whose gaze is maddeningly elsewhere. She turns to Apache, then to Billy. They both gape, but both are silent, the only sound in the room that of the dice hitting the back of the screen.

"Eight more points damage," Aron declares.

"That's it," Jack concedes with a cryptic smile.

"You killed him, Aron," Apache says, his voice quiet and accusatory.

"No, Apache," Jack says. "The orc killed Ambrosia. It's a game, remember?"

25. Stasimon: Strophe

(Enter in the orchestra CLIO, MELPOMENE, and THALIA. MELPOMENE and THALIA move to the edge of the stage, chivalrously offering a hand's down to POLYMNIA, who joins them in front and below the stage. Together, all four turn toward the spectacle behind the "magic lantern" pantomime: they watch the unfolding of events along with us, providing commentary as the players mime on stage.)

Polymnia: Like a tale told by drunks in a park, Aron Starr's story of rescue and descent builds on consent with others.

Here, when the will lies in danger, art descends and rescues, arriving as a saving, healing magician. Art alone can turn those moments of horror, or absurdity, or even resentment, into something imagined by all. Only then are all things bearable, and only then can the game continue.

We watch from the parlor along with Jack—four sisters called to an assembly, an *agon*, surrounding a pouting, translucent boy, whose comrades now begin their small rebellions. The calm of Asia, a mask to his friends, hides a turbulence—Republican and entitled and Hoosier—an anger at having been treated like this,

115

dismissed from the game and the community by concealed dice rolls, and a greater anger that he cannot return the dishonor in kind. He knows that Aron has gilded the dice rolls, so we coddle the boy, canoodling with invisible hands his face and chest and extremities, Thalia's ethereal fingers halfway up his inner thigh before Melpomene stops her sternly, as adored Jack murmurs, arches his ailurean back and falls into a doze, pampered and caressed, his copy of *Our Town* tented on his chest.

Calliope: The *agon* begins here. Together, Jack's friends rescue the moment from disgust, from absurdity.

You might say they rescue Jack himself.

Responding to the orc attack, Brendan raises his staff. You might only see Vincent, leaning across the table, gathering dice.

But notice the air buckle above him, the ambiguous shadow that might be a druid, rising to substance out of the convergence of lamplights.

At his cue—the druid's or her brother's—Melusine readies a Fireball spell, while Maia looks to the parlor, her gaze passing through me to settle on drowsing Jack, while her silhouette, cast on the Starrs' postered wall, takes on a hood and dark corona.

The other party members, Hrothgar and Kleptos (Kleptos? Apache is uninventive with names) draw their swords to face the onrush of aleatory evil.

Dice in the open, Vincent orders.

Maia nods, her eyes stern and enigmatic.

Thalia: Aron glares back at such challenges, such *lèse* to his *majesté*. But what, indeed, can he do? To hide the dice reveals his guilt, to reveal them shows the ropes and pulleys, the backstage of his illusions.

But what is his option? His shadow dwindles, he is lost in bald light as he shows forth the twenty-sided dice, the famous d20, geodesic and mysterious.

And this time the players move first, not seeing the spectral and musal hand that turns the numbers in their favor. Oh yes, we are dice loaders on the side of fair dealing, of poetic justice.

Calliope: As one, they announce their intention to absorb the first attack of Aron's invented orcs. Maia, in turn, tells us that Melusine will cast her Light spell, while Apache's Kleptos searches for escape passages in the bright, magical glow.

With their first declarations of intent, their play becomes mutinous. To Aron's dismay, Maia's dice roll is a pure, unaided 20…

Thalia: Not quite unaided, sister. But whatever…

Calliope: By this the players know that, no matter what obstacles or opposition Aron had set for them, they have surmounted his plans by Melusine's magic, which is Maia's audacious and momentary luck.

A roll like hers means that the players are at blinding advantage. But it is no competition, or is it? More a performance—a story they will all create together, as they tell themselves.

Like we have nothing to do with it.

Thalia: Or like we do.

Now Aron rolls the die, and we could tell he secretly hopes for victory, the orcs' triumph, command of the game once more. The little bitch. Doesn't know what he wants, but it isn't higher rolls on tesserae and tali, on those fancy astragaloi.

Calliope: But the die roll brings into being Melusine's magic light, and by it their shadows take on definition, borders and solidity. Or the shadows of their characters, their imagined persona thrown onto the parlor wall. There Brendan and Hrothgar are standing back to back, weapons at the ready and Kleptos crouches, adept hands feeling the surface of the Starrs' drywall for a passage to the netherworld. All of this illumined by the torch in the hand of a thin, feminine silhouette, Melusine's arms aloft as she stood above the fallen body of a comrade, as Maia bends over the table.

(The actors behind the curtain rise from their seats and adopt the narrated roles and postures.)

Melpomene: These are their constructs, whispered out of abstraction. By these, they keep living. The Sublime that masters the horrible, and the Comic that springs us away from disgust at the meaningless, the absurd. These children are our chorus, our satyrs or old men or Euripidean women, attendants of the god, saving us from nothingness by their game.

Calliope: May the luck of the dice continue and sustain them. I am sure they are clever, these puzzles of maze and code that Aron has set before them. But the gamers are buoyed now, self confident: every moment of chance this evening has fallen their way, and when you ride a current, you decide without second-guess, with intelligence of the body and the instincts rather than the entanglement of thought and self.

Polymnia: Aron runs out of prepared encounters within half an hour. Within an hour, he is too tired to improvise, and the game, which usually lasts until the wee hours, adjourns at midnight.

At another time, I might have warned them. But I know the serpent's design, or know at least that there is a design, a pattern set in motion before there was a theatre, a serpent, or even substance.

What was it Jim Morrison said, when he mistook himself for a god?

Ride the snake?

I have soared aloft with poetry and with high thought, and though I have laid my hand to many a reflection, I have found nothing stronger than the goddess Ananke. She emerged self-formed at the very beginning of time, shadowy and serpentine, coiling about the breadth of the universe, and from her first appearance, there has been no cure for her.

Melpomene: Hers is a law of stern Necessity, the immemorial ordinance of the gods made fast forever, bravely sworn and sealed.

She is the one who parents your genius falsely,

Who gives you the dry ground of poverty or region or religion,

She is the woman who tore apart Stephen Thorne, or Aron Starr. Or Lucius Sora. Or maybe Jack himself.

Behind the stage she coils. You have not seen her, but she is there.

Polymnia: When we rise, we surface from her pulse and current, in bas-relief, like figures in a frieze.

Don't you know by now? How we switch names, take a different marching order to trick beholders with our processional?

We exchange lutes, scrolls, podia. Our sarcophagus transforms, we cover our tracks, and the generations to come will guess at us, though the nine of us are one girl only, and that girl a tide in Ananke's ocean.

Melpomene: And nevertheless, all nine of us fear her in unison, fear Ananke, hungry Necessity. For if those born to enduring life should sin by slaughter, by disputation, falsehood, oath-breaking…

Thalia: In short, by the things at which we excel…

Melpomene: For three times ten thousand years they shall wander outcast from joy, condemned to mortal being, and go their ways in many shapes—in clay and stone and metal—through many hardships. The heavens will force them headlong to the Sea; and dry land receive them when they vomit forth. Unwanted they rise to the burning Sun; and then, thrown backward into the vast entropy of heaven, moving unwelcome from host to host, by all abhorred.

For a while we coil in the skin of the snake, away from the untimely spring chill, foetal beneath the stage. And even though Jack Rausch has barely noticed the podgy old men—the fanciful actor, the creature of lamé and prophecy, and the director who approached him—it might be that he understands the complicity of this triad, their unity and nullity.

But he has passed into Stephen's attentions, and though Stephen might have explained all of this as Jack's entering the story, that is not what it was at all, far from it.

If anything, it was opposite to that.

26.Stasimon: Antistrophe

(Those MUSES in the orchestra turn to face the audience. CALLIOPE shields her eyes, looks out over the amphitheater.)

Calliope: Someone is Lykourgos here. Crazy godstruck and defined by what he does not know.

Polymnia: Tell us, my epic sister, before we lose shape and substance, sublimating past vapor into aether, before we vanish to the park, the groves and statuary.

Calliope: When the Lord Dionysos set out eagerly through the kingdom of Thrace, drawing people to his cult and his worship. Lykourgos, son of Dryas and king of the Edonians, refused to bow to the god. So Dionysos fled to the sea, taking shelter with the gods of water and ocean, but his girls, his Maenads, were taken captive…

Thalia: And the Satyroi as well, the horned and goat-footed balloon men, our companions in the revels...

Calliope: So I remember. Lykourgos imprisoned them as well. But we all were freed, were we not? after which the god came to Lykourgos caped and young like his father, heavy-kneed and pouring rain like his grandpa. Now a lion, now an unbroken horse, now a bull and a tiger and at last a horned serpent, coiled in the recesses of the Edonian palace.

Melpomene: And Lykourgos saw the god thus, in scaled translation, serpentine and hungry, the thing behind the thing behind the thing?

Calliope: Heard the dark and skittering rustle over his marbled floors. Smelled the copper and the stagnancy of water. The god obscured like *élan vital* pushed down, down, until it emerges hysterical, until it must be answered.

Lykourgos smelled the serpent, and straightway he heard the rupture of our bars, our chains, as the god set us free and we scattered to vantage points in the shoreline rocks, where we saw the god rise from the sea in form divine and unbearable, trailing weeds and aether. And Lykourgos on the shoreline, shaking with fear, for he saw the glorious son of Zeus, and pale terror fell on him. Now the ox-goad, with which he had chased the god into the waters, fell useless from the king's hand, and his strong will left him. Still he might have escaped, but when Dionysos approached, he stood in defiance

Melpomene: So he urged us then, did the god—urged maenad, satyr and muse—to scourge Lykourgos with rods and branches.

Thalia: I remember how his dark skin opened like blossoms.

Calliope: Still he stood (did he not?) like a rock against which both wind and sea break uselessly. The king had gone too far. He was king and could do nothing but stand, his mantle and crown too heavy for movement. Then rage settled on the heart of Semele's son, and he vowed that slow revenge was better than sudden death.

Madness the god sent upon Lykourgos, and the phantom shapes of serpents, until Lykourgos' two sons and his wife came before the king. Foolish boys, they cast their arms around their father, but he, thinking them serpents, struck them dead. In compassion Lord Dionysos swept the wife beyond the reach of doom, yet Lykourgos remained unflinching. So the god spread vines about him, entangling his limbs, neckbone snapping in the pressure of branches.

Muses: And now in the land of shades his phantom draws water from the flow of the Acheron. Such the punishment ordained for men who fight against the gods; that retribution follow them living and dead.

27. Stasimon: Antistrophe

(POLYMNIA, THALIA, MELPOMENE, AND ERATO *move to the four corners of the stage. The remaining MUSES step backward, upstage, half in shadow)*

Muses: Four dreams of four sisters, afloat in the spring air along the court, taking substance in gaslight and humidity. Each of the dreams framing a dream, story within story as the god bursts his shackles.

Thalia: In the park lies a fat man covered in lamé and newspaper. Who dreams as well, snoring wine-lulled in the shadows of the park, imagining himself prone and belly-up on the boards of the stage as a slim dark figure approaches through his dream. A boy, dark haired and vaguely Asian, vaguely familiar as he takes on body and features. He is rising from the light of the court, which shines behind him as though he had the sun at his back and circled above the dreamer, ready to swoop down the tiered rows of the amphitheater.

And *Jesus*, thinks the fat man. *Where the hell is it I know him from?* his tipsy thoughts ranging back over a decade's wandering the park, further still as the trees seemed to shrink to saplings behind the hovering boy and then rise again, no longer the domesticated, manicured Olmstead foliage but something disheveled and wild, plant life he feels he should remember but doesn't quite, as it burgeons and blossoms in a spring so ancient there is even a cavernous cool on the breeze of receding glaciers, of a time not familiar to history or language or even human knowing…

And *Jesus*, the fat man thinks, which makes me smile until my face resembles my mask.

Erato: Here lies an older man, asleep in silks in a high ceilinged apartment on the court. At first he dreams only of his room and the court surrounding it, as though he might pass into waking by crossing the thinnest of membranes, a veil between worlds.

And it seems that the same boy has just passed out of his dream, headed toward the shadows and the park beyond Magnolia Street, as the older man watches him go. If the boy looks vaguely familiar to T. Tommy Briscoe, it is to George Castille that he seems downright pronounced and memorable. It is and is not Jack Rausch: of that he is sure. Those dark and delicate good looks that broke hearts back in the day—breaking George Castille's now, in the land of dreaming—as the boy gives a last glance over his shoulder before the shade engulfs him.

Something Orphic and doomed about him, something passing from the bright land of the living into unknown country, but at the same time there is in his bearing a new swagger and menace, which George finds arousing, despite having sworn off the young ones.

My ambition is not so high, he whispers. Now he is *eidolon* or *simulacrum*. For Castille's dreamboy is the mask and the player through which pass my sister's thoughts and breathing, and behind her insufflations the breath of the god.

So much for satyrs, for beautiful lads in troops, thinks George Castille. *As for me, I am the one who has never faltered, who has seen the beautiful come and go, who has denied himself and served the mind instead of the body. Oh, give me this one, god of dreams and secret yearning, give me this one as he passes through the gates of ivory.*

And the boy looks back at him, eyes delicately angled and dark. Splendor flashes from him, like the moon emergent from the fog, and George Castille surrenders his dignity, crying out in the dappled and humbled night.

Polymnia: And here is the dream I had, youngest of sisters, a dream of the clergyman turning restless on his bed, his wife a stillness in hairspray and cologne. Again the devil, goat-footed and horned and bearded, comes to the mat for him, the grip unspeakable and searing, the minister's arms clawed back until his chest throbs and threatens to burst with the exertion of breaking the hold. And the devil tells him a story: that the god was born of union with god and mortal, was torn in pieces, and having died, he rose again, and ascended to heaven, leaving wine and the broken flesh in his mysteries.

The pastor joins hands behind the knotted, caprine back, knots his fingers, squeezes and lofts the creature, who clamps his wrist firmly, pulling his arm free and behind him. Now he falls, the devil spread-eagled on his naked belly, until, fixing the soles of his feet to the ground, the minister pushes up and away, and both roll across the floor, sweaty and struggling and somehow compliant, the creature pressing on the Reverend Peter Koenig, jackhammering his chest until his heart ossifies, his word and breath and dreaming leave him, and *Euoi!* The old Silenoi shout...

As *calfrope*, the devil breathes, the old country way to ask for surrender, to say uncle. *Calf rope. Say calf rope.*

Melpomene: A last and feminine call to the boy, as Dolores stands by the window, her hand gesturing figures on the glass. She sees the boy on the stage, a legion of disheveled women leading forth a garlanded bull. From afar the women say,

Muses: Come this way, and I will make you famous on his back, and the gods will applaud you loudly. There is nothing to fear; Europa was but a girl, and she made this ride, bareback and without reins.

Melpomene: Dolores watches as the boy stands over the bull's brow, stroking the curved horns and excited by a sweet sting of desire and fear. The women deck the bull's body with fresh dewy leaves, they wreath red roses about his back, lift lilies and daffodils over his brow and a ring of purple anemone on his neck. Now the boy calls out, boasting to the round Moon, and the bull, goaded by moonlight, wanders the trackless grounds of the park.

So rode the boy as the bull gathers fury. Dolores calls out to him, forgetting he is an image, simulacrum and eidolon. The bull lowers its horns and bucks, and the youth on its back clings vainly, his shoulders bunching, growing larger, more definite, a shape his mother knows as well as her own as he hurtles through streetlight and she hears and does not hear the sound of his fall and breaking.

His blood flows like forbidden vintage. Against her instinct and nature, she savors it.

Muses: And in four beds in four places, sleepers startle awake, and something in the world shifts as the god begins to move. And as he moves, so ends the first act of the story. Set it down, rest your eyes.

Smoke 'em if you got 'em.

28. Episode: Best-Laid Plans

Polymnia: Vincent De Chevre opens his eyes and laughs.

His sister is in the bathroom. The sound of her hair dryer usually comforts him with its familiarity, even as it jostles him toward wakefulness. But this morning he is wide alert, attuned to notions. Banging on the bathroom door, he reminds her of their undercover rescue plot, and Maia De Chevre, usually the more cautious and demure of the twins, whoops in agreement.

She chooses to overlook the obstacles. How they can expect help only from Billy and Apache. How Aron will no doubt balk at the plan, and how Stephen Thorne and perhaps even George Castille will be horrified. Still she mulls and savors the scheme, turning on the dryer again, her hair crackling under the hot rush and the electric roar. She thinks of the adventure, the chance for disguise and secret agency, the most awesome casting call for a play in theatre history. The old hippies will get with the program later, because if Stephen Thorne prides himself on subversive theatre, this shit was downright guerrilla: if he is as good as the game he talks, he will see the poetry in public kidnapping.

Aron is the problem, she knows. Maia has watched him watch them, peeping tom as she and Jack sat on the stage and exchanged histories. Aware of Aron's gaze that night, she had touched Jack's arm frequently in the conversation. Had once leaned in, laughed, and rested her head briefly on his shoulder. And no, it was not all about sending Aron mixed signals but *unmixing* them. If he doesn't know (as surely he should by now) he *needs* to know that this watching her from distances has a creepy edge to it, that there is such a thing as imaginary stalking, an obsession that sometimes slides into the visible and real.

It is testament to Aron Starr's timidity that he has not and will not step front stage to serenade her, but simply stare yearningly from somewhere in the wings. He is timid in too many things, and since her brother's plan demands a sense of venture, and since the goal is to rescue Jack from Antioch and *Our Town*, Maia doubts that Aron will go along. At least until she's had a crack at him, a chance to pitch and explain the kidnap plan she and Vincent had worked up over wine and reefer last night.

On the other hand, Jack Rausch will come willingly. She knows it from the look of him, and from the way he talked to her on top of Hamlet's castle. For a moment she startles, as a glance in the mirror reveals me staring back at the recesses of sight. She has that moment of hovering, as the reflection clears and I back away, and no longer is there anyone behind her. The play will be the thing, indeed, and she hopes to catch more than the conscience of luminous Jack.

29. Proagon: Choregos ex Machina

(The choruses assemble: THE MUSES in the orchestra, stage right, where POLYMNIA descends to join them, and T. TOMMY BRISCOE and THE BRISCHORDS, filing in stage left. They look up toward the rafters where, slowly, a green porch swing, festooned with vines and plastic grapes, is lowered, seated upon it THE CHOREGOS, a dumpy, white-haired Irishman in his late fifties. Halfway down, the swing hitches and stalls at a slant, and THE CHOREGOS slides to one end, clutching the arm rest nervously and looking down to the stage.)

Tommy: Is this the *deus ex machina*, children? The god we've been waiting for?

Falcon: The *deus ex machina*? Explain...

Tommy: "The god from the machine". Back in the day, when the play had got itself in a fix, when there was no way for the heroes to get out of a tight spot, the god would come down to sort things out. Usually Apollo or Athena done the main work, because they're the smartest gods, but others might of pitched in when the problems rose.

Thalia (dryly): Not much of a *deus…*

Tommy: Not much of a *machina.*

Choregos: It's wonderful up in this swing.

(Swings out over the stage).

I can look to my left and see all the way to the overpass, to the brief tunnel of dark that led you into the city almost fifty years ago, that one night bristled with a guard of statuary. And in front of me, over a stand of trees, I can see almost all the way to Ninth Street, to the spot where poor Syrine was unraveled and where the big cat stalks. Behind me, masked in blinding, prohibitive light during the day and by trees and shadow of trees when dusk falls over Eastern Parkway, there is the country where the goatboy and his progeny haunt the creekside, and north, to my right and beyond Broadway, among the city lights and bustle of pedestrians, the Shangri-La Theatre opens its doors and the ghosts retreat to the alcoves and balconies because it is not their season, not yet.

From its spacious and sculpted eastern neighborhoods, home to its movers and shakers, to its declining, gaudy downtown, the city eats its young. It nurtures its arrivistes, while it fails its homegrown artists and starves its native scholars, depending on where in the great and secretly mapped urban ground they are born and grow up: from its south end would-be novelists to the actors born in the sprawl of its suburbs, to the singers and musicians that haunt its westernmost streets to the painter just north of the river, whose images mold and crumble in neglected basements. It is where they all go to die in separate, desperate careenings across the wheels within wheels that move just under the surface of the city like a thwarted clockwork grinding down and away.

It's beautiful, and sad, and too much to watch. Someone give me a hand here?

(MUSES and BRISCHORDS applaud).

No, no, you smartasses. A hand *down*.

(D.J. Mel helps the old fellow descend).

Much better. I hate to disappoint you, but I'm no *deus*. Just a humble *choregos*, coming down for my moment in the play.

Falcon: I'll bite. What's a *choregos*?

Tommy: I got nothing. Girls?

(Pause)

Melpomene *(sighs)*: Much like your producer. The *choregos* gets the cast together, schedules the play, foots the bill.

Choregos: Sort of like Thorne and Castille, except the two of them are fictional. I'm at least partially fact.

(TOMMY sits on the edge of the stage).

Tommy: So, where are we headed, boss? What twists of plot and tomfoolery are up the road? And is everything going to be all right for Maia and Aron and lovely Jack?

Choregos: It's The Bacchae, Tommy. It's a tragedy. Things will not end well.

"Not *Our Town.* Not *Blade Runner.*"

"But it's our City," The Choregos tells Tommy "Sorry about the river"

30. Agon: As the Muses Watch

Polymnia: It is all craziness according to Aron Starr.

Everyone meets at his place, over the game, and, as Maia has predicted, he is the last sentient being to hold out.

We arrive before the mortals. Melpomene and Thalia, in their idea of a joke, slide ethereally behind the dramatic masks that Dolores Starr keeps on her wall as conversation pieces nobody ever talks about. They think it is especially funny that Melpomene's mask is smiling and Thalia's tearful, though I keep telling them that such humor is too broad and obvious. So two of my sisters wait and bicker in silence, while others get busy.

Billy and Apache join readily in Vincent's plan, Erato having seduced their dreams. A boy can be drawn by his dick into all kinds of adventure, so we give them images, mostly centered on Maia and the gullibilities of Baptist girls.

But Aron, cool and resistant, ever the game-master mapping escapade, points out the silliness of the venture.

Clio: Antioch Baptist Church is a kind of fortress against the world. Rehearsals at its theatre are protected, as are the children who perform in its family-friendly dramas—protected according to the principle that the world out there is made up of all kinds of seductions, and you know what happens.

Polymnia: It makes the Baptists tighten security, Aron argues. Would make nigh impossible what his friends want to do.

Furthermore, Aron doesn't see why everyone wants to kidnap Jack Rausch. It will stir up commotion, he says, and give that Bible-thumping bunch something to rampage about, not that they need it. Jack might or might not come willingly, and if he doesn't, this is kidnapping for real, a punishable crime, don't you all know?

But even if Jack goes along, what do they plan to do once they have him?

So arguments begin, until we settle over them all. Breathed spirit into their ambitions.

Now Vincent points out the boy's charisma. That it is more than dice rolls in a game, in case Aron has forgotten. Girls like Jack, and there is something about him: he will stand well in the chorus, perhaps even lead it.

You have completely forgotten, Aron replies, that the chorus is women, and even if Jack Rausch likes that kind of thing I can't imagine our chorus leader in drag…

To which the boys all laugh, reminding him that this was Euripides, that the women in Greek drama were played by men.

And embarrassed, cornered by ridicule, Aron asks if that was Mr. Castille's idea, because you know,

And no, Billy says, not at all, and don't be a homophobe, Aron, or we will simply trade you for Jack. And Mr. Castille will be here soon, and do you want him to hear what you said?

But Aron is no longer listening, because he is angered no end—the part about trading him for Jack, as Thalia figured it would when she whispered the barb to Billy.

So now comes time for Maia to intervene.

We want him here for good reason, Aron, she urges. You know Jack plays bass, and does it well: he's been jammin' for weeks with Vinnie, and they might even put together a band in the fall. But you also know that, right now, the play needs original music, not some CD of *Qawwali* like the dude sang with Eddie Vedder, or like the Ravi Shankar shit that Mr. Thorne got high to in the '60s.

And Aron beginning to smile because she is right and she is funny, and they all have thought it, and Maia makes him smile no matter what she says.

Thalia: We have all nudged him into tactics by the time George Castille arrives. George seems distracted. Beaten down or a little shaken at the foundations. And at first, he says no to the enterprise.

But the girls have laid the groundwork, my sisters and Maia. We have worked on him. He hates *Our Town* and Baptists, but like Aron before him, he first sees no point in a kidnapping venture.

He softens, however, at the prospect of comic disguise.

Maia is bold as a tenth muse of Rhetoric. Though none of them have met the Reverend Peter Koenig, Maia paints him in dragon colors, his school as a kind of locked stables that imprisons the god and the winged horse. Koenig is, they think, a confirmed hater of Catholics, women, gender-benders and Harry Potter—the kind of sweeping condemnation that gives them an easy villain and earns them convenient grounds for agreement whenever they gather. And there is nothing ill about Koenig and Antioch Baptist that George Castille will not believe, and by the time Maia is done with describing and we have filled him with insufflations of liberal and libertarian righteousness, the old actor hops in on the ground floor of the conspiracy.

He is cautious enough, however, to step away from it. Several times he reminds them that *the abduction part of the venture*, as he calls it, must be conceived and performed by students. When it came to lending a hand with that undertaking, he would love to, but he doesn't want to.

Polymnia: The cast agree and say they understand. They run through the evening's reading, which has improved on all fronts except Aron's Dionysus. George listens in silence because part of him has given up, while the other part drifted unsettled through last night's dreaming. And when he steps out for a smoke, Vincent and Maia produced the copies of the other play, distributed it to Aron, Apache, and Billy with a kind of submerged hilarity.

The questions of *why* will be answered later by the twins, as the whole party met to conspire over questions of *how.* Vincent whispers not to worry, that it would not have to be just the five of them. He has enlisted other help, he said, but cannot explain before George Castille comes back into the room, smelling of tobacco and instruction, having purposefully forgotten that once rehearsals were over, his cast is bound for felony.

31. Parabasis: A Tour of Mothers

Enter TOMMY BRISCOE and THE BRISCHORDS. They stand downstage left as THE MUSES move downstage right. They face one another on stage, regarding their counterparts with curiosity, but not with malice.

Polymnia: Jack visits his mother because of her capacity for noise.

He is not told this, and the Rausches frame the trips to see Beverly Nguyen as gestures of kindness and a nod to biology.

Although he is of driving age now, Jack is never allowed to make the trip on his own. Chauffeured by the Congressman's driver, he is turned and taken a roundabout path on the way to his mother. There she gives him cold coffee and *bahn choux*, assures him that she had given him up for adoption because the Rausches could provide what a child deserved. That his father, some boy named Donny Sabathia, had been killed in the first Bush war, leaving a pregnant girlfriend who no longer could keep the baby. That knowing this, she had set the child afloat on a river of dreams, downstream toward the palaces of the man for whom she worked, whose vision of America could be admired by a daughter of immigrants.

Jack listens, aware it was a lie and loving her for making a story to guard him. Out of the whispers of aunts and the surveillance of chauffeurs and state troopers, he has an idea who his father is. Has seen through that much of Beverly's fictions, leaves each visit with her embraces and manufactured tears. His soul has grown away from hers: she knows him only through conjecture and myth.

She cries at the idea of him, and he visits the idea of her, and on those grounds they make affectionate truce.

Clio: But what he does not know is this.

Before Rausch, before she joined the campaign—indeed, while Bucky Trabue was recruiting her for an internship, Beverly Nguyen had unsettling dreams.

Thalia: But don't we all, dear sister? Don't we all?

Clio: Do not dilute her dream. It is one we do not share, because our nights are long and dreamless, while hers...

Melpomene: Yes, hers are plot-essential. Even if she forgets it when she awakens.

Clio: In the small apartment down in the South End, where she shares residence with her parents and four brothers, Beverly has a corner bed to herself, a cramped and halcyon spot she imagines as hers alone.

Melpomene: But she is not alone. And that is never a solace. Our dreams are a haunted stage. Lares and manes, lemures and muses, their forms interchangeable in the theater's half-light.

Clio: She does not even dream of Rausch. Instead, it is a wind that passes over her, fiery from the east, bearing upon it the low growl of the savannah, the hot stink of blood and predation.

For a moment she is scared, lying spread-eagled among the household gods. For a moment she thinks of Rausch, his fumbled attentions, but at once the old man dissolves into shadow, and there is only the dark and the hot wind, insistent, overpowering…

Terrified, she surrenders, lifts her knees. She will remember none of this violence. Therefore will not tell dear Jack, in this sunlit room smelling of flowers and tea and attentions.

Melpomene: While Jack Rausch is receiving his mother's baffled welcome, Aron would have given his child support to imagine a fallen warrior as his own father.

His father has a nice suburban home, and Aron has a young stepmother and two toddler stepbrothers he still can't tell apart. He insists on the "step" when he mentions them: it is a way to manufacture the distance he needs.

Robert Starr's house is a place of dispersed attentions, starkly in contrast with Dolores' domineering world, but not better, not really.

Clio: When Aron was younger, he had hated organized sports, his brief, horrible visits to church, his three weeks in the Boy Scouts. Fortunately, all those attachments were short-lived, when his mother lost interest in her own role of soccer mom.

But in the theatre they had joined their desires.

His first costume had fit, had left the feel of forced stitches and cheap velour all along his arms. He was MacDuff's child, and he practiced his three lines like he was some kind of Hamlet. At the time he thought that he would never take off that costume, that he would always speak immortal lines and be changed by the speaking of them. And it did not matter to him that he forgot the lines a week after the play had closed: love of the spotlight had bonded him with his mother, as they both looked to the magic that transformed them into someone else.

TOMMY BRISCOE steps forward from the other side of the stage.

Tommy: While Aron Starr basked in his mother's attentions, wore the children's costumes and wrangled for speaking parts in her productions, Stephen Thorne has outgrowed all of that, and come to an age where he welcomes neglect.

He's grateful for Caller-ID, for his mother's fear of the city that kept her suburban and distant. He picks up the phone on occasion because that, too, is an actor's role, a costume in a performance that makes him feel cleaner, makes the whiskey taste a little better for his efforts.

This day, though, would make for more whiskey. There were lines in the Thirty-first Hexagram, one he had just been puzzling through, when all of a sudden the phone rang.

Muriel is on about the chorus. How homeless men are unreliable, prone to violence. How it might not be this way for his friends, but for *hers* the presence of vagrants will be poisonous, a gate-killer. How she had seen the type when she visited him that time (what was it?) a year ago, and how Stephen has no idea what he was in for.

He could benefit from her experience, she tells him. And it was just like him to forego wisdom.

He and I have been in conversation, though. Down to the theater. And I have impressed him, I think, with my civic-mindedness and propriety. So he calms her, lies to her that he will consider her advice, and backs her off the phone. Then returning to the I Ching, taking a breath to steady himself, he reads the commentary again.

> *Nine at the top means:*
> *The king uses him to march forth and chastise:*
> *Then it is best to kill the leaders*

And take captive the followers. No blame.

He refreshes his whiskey and digs into his desk drawer for a short, consolatory bag of reefer. He considers himself a chastiser. That part was easy. And perhaps the *killing* and the *taking captive* had to do with the brewing play.

Surely that is it. The smallness of the city has imprisoned him, and the time for release is coming. The play is a kind of liberation, he thinks—liberation in all of its disobedience and mayhem. And the casting is making the prospects better all the time.

Surely the chorus will cut him free of bonds.

That's his story, children. And he's sticking to it.

32. Episode: The King of Antioch

Manent POLYMNIA; exeunt TOMMY and THE BRISCHORDS, the rest of THE MUSES. POLYMNIA stands center stage.

Polymnia: As *Our Town* prepares production at the Antioch Baptist Church, my sisters revert to cold marble, their positions changing once again in the procession. Outside the glass casing and the climatically sealed museum, the temperature rises and the weather becomes unstable.

This city hugs the river as though it is wringing the last moisture from it. When the summer comes, windows and eyeglasses steam over when you step outside before noon. By June, the visitors come into the museum in a haze of condensation and morning sweat, and they are thankful for the cool.

It is worse by the river, of course, but relentless throughout the town. Even its gated and manorial eastern suburbs shimmer like mirages when the temperature slides toward sweltering. The old neighborhoods are run-down but better in summer weather, with their century-old trees and vertical town-house shadows.

But wherever you go, it is hot in Louisville.

Day after day, the chariot drives through the spaces of heaven, the god's golden hair flowing wildly in a wind out of the east. And people go inside. They incline to laziness and spectator sports. And the sun gives way to humid and excessive night.

Sunday mornings, even before the heat becomes uncomfortable, a caravan of yellow buses coasts in irregular traffic down the main north-south thoroughfare, on I-65 until a southeast neighborhood opens into the demesne of Antioch Baptist Church, grounds spread over both sides of the interstate so that returning Jesus might have a wide landing strip in case his copilot was neither all-powerful nor all-seeing.

Churches for singles and couples, for *seniors* and *the youth*. For families and for those who have yet to breed.

In all of these echelons, the Reverend Peter Koenig ranks high.

Koenig is in charge of dramatic productions, though he never visits the stage. After all, old notions died hard about the theater's counterfeit, and as he justifies the plays as pageant and instruction—sometimes as wholesome entertainment—Koenig understands why it took his faith so long to bury actors on holy ground.

All that said and done, he likes the theater himself, and he and his wife Maraleese have found their way quietly into secluded seats in the city's downtown venues. If he runs into a church member in the lobby, their conversation is quiet but unembarrassed.

But if there was a play to produce on church grounds, it has to be something like *Our Town*.

Some things remain a little hard to address at Antioch: *Midsummer Night's Dream* is too bawdy, not to mention its brush with the supernatural. *Harvey*, as well. The supernatural part, that is. And *Death of a Salesman* criticizes the American Way of Life, while *Miracle Worker* features uncomfortable people.

Koenig hates the whole whitewashed image of living that makes for avoiding, for fugitive and cloistered virtue. And yet the sick modern soul, the melancholy spirit, seem unmanly and diseased. People grub in rat-holes instead of living in the light. They manufacture fears, major on every unwholesome kind of misery. Between that and happy evasion, Koenig finds himself slightly more liable to prefer the light.

There is a scene, though, in *Our Town*, that always troubles him—a moment when the Stage Manager is asked, by two rather shrill inquisitors, whether the town has a place for the pursuit of social justice or artistic beauty: his answer to both, a kind of *aw shucks, I reckon we get by as best we can*, is more an accusation than answer. It is like the questioners are suspects just for asking.

It makes Koenig wonder when he had passed from challenging things he didn't like into defending things he didn't particularly care for. Seminary school, maybe. Or maybe his first church here in town, for he is not from here, like Antioch's flock of imports. Louisville, however, has become his town, their town. Our Town. Writ large and at the turn of a different century but hankering back to times previous like a humid, river-swamped Grover's Corners.

Not long after he arrived here to attend seminary, Koenig had seen a film, already a decade old, called *Louisville: City of the Seventies*. And now, the millennial year long past, the title is still appropriate. Segregated largely by race and almost entirely by class, it is a cluster of small towns, balkanized by high school districts that have everything to do with who you are. He looks out at his congregation, 15,000 on a good Sunday, and figures you could draw a crowd that large and that overwhelmingly white only at a Stanley Cup game.

Not only the whiteness troubles him, though. Antioch is too big for his tastes these days. There is less and less of a personal touch, he figures, in the ministrations of half a dozen assistant pastors. He has always found more room for God with the accoutrements stripped away, with the friction of soul against soul.

Roy Rausch's phone call, forwarded that morning, has created a different friction of its own. Resentful at being put on hold while Koenig pursued what he claimed were other pastoral concerns but was actually a sandwich order, the State Representative grumbled through arranging a counseling appointment for his nephew Jack, a principal actor in *Our Town*.

The boy was supposedly adopted from somewhere in Asia. But people said that the Rausch lineaments and lineage were apparent, and everyone's silent guess was that Roy was the father.

If Rausch had been a Democrat, it would have been the talk of the church.

Koenig walks to the front of his desk. He never greets visitors from behind it. Now, waiting for Jack Rausch to enter, he turns toward the print on the wall—a reproduction of Rubens' *Christ's Entry into Jerusalem*. He has been told the painting is "too Catholic" by someone with a lot of money, but he has held his ground and kept it in the office. Now he places his hands in his pockets and smiles at the almost frenzied pace of the piece, Our Lord and Savior riding the donkey like a hulking jockey in the midst of a gauntlet of palm fronds, the beginning of the Passion in some crowded rush, the celebrants crouched muscular around the outsized rider, encircling Him, fanning Him, spreading branches and clothing in His path, for *Blessed be the King that cometh in the name of the Lord*, Peter Koenig whispers, the verse from Luke that they always quoted on Palm Sunday.

Peter hears the door open in the outer office, the pleasant and saccharine greeting Maraleese used in her secretarial role, a polite young male voice in response. And a darker verse comes to mind. *And when he was come near, he beheld the city, and wept over it, Saying, If thou hadst known, even thou, at least in this thy day, the things which belong unto thy peace! but now they are hid from thine eyes.*

Each young person to come into Peter Koenig's office is a cartouche.

The staff and younger clergy frown when he says that, but only because they do not know the word. Not because it wasn't so.

The cartouche, Koenig always explains, is the oval in Egyptian inscriptions. It indicates that the text inside is a royal name. It shades how you read the hieroglyphs, the signs, creating meaning by sound, by the associations with each picture, by how those pictures speak to each other.

This makes for complex translation, he tells them. He confesses that he did not know first-hand, but that others— experts in the field—had told him so in seminary. It seems that the signs mean a number of things simultaneously, like the intents and motives of people.

Those blurred intents and motives are why Peter Koenig keeps open his office doors during all conferences. Why his wife was his secretary. His protection, like the elliptical border of the cartouche, is designed to fend and ward off evil.

With dangers set aside, Koenig can read in comfort the faces and gestures of advisees, move beyond what is said into what is meant, the difficult translation of counseling. It had been Bob Dylan, if he remembered rightly, who had talked about how

Your debutante knows what you need
But I know what you want.

Jack Rausch is a surprise, though. The children of moneyed church people tend toward entitlement, but Jack sits only when invited, regards Koenig with a level, friendly gaze, and nods at the right times when the clergyman speaks. Koenig suspects performance, of course, and watches the boy's face for tells, for giveaways, but it is a mask that looks back at him.

Koenig explains why it might be unwise to spend time with more theatrical people. He hopes that he didn't sound too much like Roy Rausch as he explained. Theatre people, he says, tend to magnify things. To expand the situation until you don't recognize the emotion, or you lose its meaning. He had dated a local actress for a while, he confides to Jack, back before seminary. He had learned his lesson, because you know how girls turn things upside down.

Man to man, he tries, because of course Roy Rausch was most afraid that the boy's sexuality wasn't right, because after all, look at him.

And now, Peter Koenig is looking, and he notices nothing that would mark Jack Rausch as inverted. No mannerism, no reedy and feminine tone to the voice, though Koenig knows that these things are not always present where the problem lies, and sometimes, they are present without the problem, as they are in Antioch's happily married music minister, Tarquin LaForce.

Instead, the boy is charismatic, almost blindingly so, and Koenig wrestles his thoughts into the wish that Jack might be called to the clergy. Indeed, he nudges the conversation in that direction, but soon realizes that Jack has no interest in the ministry or in ministerial advice.

It isn't that he frowns, or looks away, or gives any sign of dissent. Instead he sits impassive as a *kouros*, one of those archaic Greek statues of a young man—no particular young man, but any young man, or better yet, the embodiment of male beauty, his musculature not incised, not defined, but a kind of geometric shaping that inclines toward the abstract...

As Koenig catches himself in mid-speculation, his eyes lock on the boy's dark gaze, and he could tell Jack looks through him or beyond him, toward whatever vanishing point lies in or behind the painting above them, to where the reproduced brush-strokes of the Rubens copy lose themselves in the halo of Christ.

Are you listening? he asks, and *why, yes sir,* the boy replies. *But these people, you see, are musical friends, and gaming friends...*

Koenig frowns, and believes Jack must recall what Antioch thinks of role-playing games, because the boy's story shifts ground to a conversation about playing bass with Vincent De Chevre...

Then away from music as well. Elusive, as though he recognizes that there isn't much he is doing with his new friends that will meet the official approval of Peter Koenig. Who dismisses him with kind but cautionary words, and after the boy leaves the office, pivots his chair toward the image of Jesus emergent from a grove of palm fronds and hands.

Jack Rausch seems other than the things he does. There is something behind the music and theatre and gaming that Peter Koenig cannot decipher, a kind of disinterest that jars the eye. *Disinterest*, he reminds himself. *Not lack of interest.*

For the boy's eyes had been intent, though focused elsewhere. And the concealed impatient drumming of his fingers across the pastoral desk as he stood to leave was a sign that he had finished something, that he had weathered some trial and, in his *disinterest*, judged himself to have passed some kind of audition.

An audition that the minister fears he has failed. For when Jack leaves the room to Maraleese Koenig's sweet goodbyes, Peter Koenig feels a grip loosen on his chest. Not of danger or of ill will, but of sheer and indifferent power, that washes over and through him like a current he had been swimming against. And something tells him he should be afraid for Jack Rausch, while something stronger intimates that Jack is not the one in peril.

For only the second time in twenty years, Peter is tempted to call Dolores Starr. Theatre people are her people, and surely she would know something about the boy.

He guesses she has a new phone number by now.

She has a son, too.

He stared straight into the heart of the painting. Does sums on his fingers, and sits back reassured.

Briefly his small bark steadies in the flow of an ineluctable current, and the Reverend Peter Koenig assures himself with math and the fringes of faith.

33. Episode: Dolores Dines Alone

The grill marks on the steak run in one direction only.

Because these days she turns the meat immediately, and only once.

The steak sits on her plate now, a mottled brown-gray pooled with pink juices, streaked across with four unbroken lines atop two split by a mottled vein of fat.

Dolores stifles a giggle, drains her glass of wine.

It is like one of Stephen's hexagrams. His silly rituals of rock star Buddhism and New Age greenness. She never understood it back then, at least no more than she understood a man twice her age and his interest in a high school girl.

All she had figured was that it was a matter of counting. A kind of Taoist jugglery with the yarrow stalks. Counting off by fours the numbers of stalks in your hand, moving back and forth from hand to hand, apportioning little bundles that looked mysterious, as though the wind could pass through them and create unheard melodies.

Though how an unheard melody would sound, she could not imagine at sixteen. She had watched Stephen in the process of consulting the I Ching, and at first it had been one of his appeals. It gave him youth and a kind of exotic turn, even if he was only her high-school drama teacher, inclining toward the weight he would carry twenty years later, and helpless before his mother's transgression and acid.

Now, early in her own middle age, Dolores forgives those shortcomings, understands and lives them all. The prophecies of the I Ching, though, returned to her in a fascinating circle when she saw the yarrow stalks scattered on Stephen's table those evenings they all discussed the play. She wonders why he had kept at it all these years, and yet she is not inclined to ask, feeling that she might give him the wrong ideas.

She bends over the steak. Carves the first bite and examined the gelid red between the papery brown layers. Just enough to tell herself she cooked it.

She pours a second glass of Merlot.

Early on, trying to explain the oracle, Stephen had told her about the changing lines. Old yin and old yang. She could not follow the mathematics, his talk of probabilities and remainders, of multiple coins, of dice and beads. She suspected that he knew as little about them as she did, that he was all talk when it came to this, like he was in other things. But what she did understand was that the old lines were unstable, the young ones steady. That in the process of aging, the lines transform until they become their opposite—old yang to young yin, old yin to young yang, forming a new hexagram, a new insight as they change.

Now she understands the comfort of her teaching job, the daily expectations, the new things taking place in familiar structures. She is onto the second wave of students—kids whose mothers or fathers she has taught. Consoles herself that generations passed quickly in the city, that she is no older because teenagers dropped out of high school to breed. It is good to pretend to be surprised by their insights, to see them grow like their mothers had, especially when the growth is old ground to her and vastly new and wonderful to them, a kind of best of both worlds.

Stephen had told her once that when you used the yarrow stalks to consult the I Ching, it moves the lines differently. The coins were binary, he said, heads or tails. So yin and yang were equally likely. But the stalks showed a stable yin, an active yang moving slowly, over months and years and centuries, toward its stationary and passive counterpart. Dolores is all right with that, with movement that is a kind of banking of energies, that suggests how eventually we settle into something more thoroughly ourselves.

But what works for her works less well for the men she knew. Stephen has become what she suspected he would after several years around him—a pot-smoking refugee from America's silliest decade, an indulged Boomer who had yet to learn the lesson his generation still worked through, that they were not so special, not really.

And her time with Peter Koenig a mystery when she met him for coffee after the recent phone call, when he *asked her for advice,* of all things. Called in by Jack Rausch's father to consult on the boy's well-being, Koenig was still a presence like he'd been in the old days, but changed as well, jowls and staid demeanor covering the passion of the young seminarian she had dated briefly until they both discovered, almost by mutual consent, that the distance between their worlds could not be spanned by anything but the most ardent affections, which at that time he had devoted to Jesus and she to the theatre, both of them sure that their truths would make them whole and authentic. Now he troops the high school halls (and, she expected, his offices at the church, and she would find out for herself soon) with a kind of respectability you wore like a costume, gestures of cultural and Biblical confidence, and she reckons the strong lines of his search had led to an established peace, though how it would be peace she cannot figure.

She washes down the last morsel of the meat with the last swallow of wine. At least the last from this glass.

She pours the third and thinks of Aron. Her own son has passed through sullen country on his way from yang to yin. Or is still passing through it. And though it annoys her that Aron has not arrived in a place that was good for him, that he still mopes through activities, is secretive and putting on pounds, she tells herself it is part of the process, his changing lines.

But she wants more from him.

His father's genes, she tells herself with uncertainty. Some things hold you back.

The fourth glass goes down smoothly. She hopes she has another bottle.

Nevertheless, Dolores tells herself, Aron should have shown signs of his election by now. He should have displayed the gifts she was certain he would have when she knew it was a boy she carried, and later when that boy moved the first time in her belly. He is already bound somewhere, she knows, and sometimes on nights like this, made speculative by wine, she stands above his bed and watches this hulking, teen-aged enigma, thrashing under his blanket and drooling onto the sheets. She takes in hand his pillow, imagines stillness, silence, the long prospect of solitude, and again she wonders how she has come to this, how she has changed.

34. Stasimon: Strophe: T. Tommy and the Brischords

T. Tommy: Up there. Top of the slope. It was Hamlet's stage last year. Where he took on his mother, after the play. Not after *Hamlet*, but after the play in Hamlet, the trap in the middle of it, where the theatre sprung and opened its maw for the old king, like the jaws of a bear trap or a python. Hamlet held the mirror up to her then.

He told her,

> Sit you down; you shall not budge;
> You go not till I set you up a glass
> Where you may see the inmost part of you.

And what was it she told him? What mother's words back to the son?

O Hamlet, speak no more:
Thou turn'st mine eyes into my very soul;
And there I see such black and grained spots
As will not leave their tinct.

Into her soul. What she said, children.

Because it was never that the boy could not make up his mind. He right well done so when he did not act. Your Hamlet turned his eyes inward, and he understood.

Because he could not change the tide of things, and he knew it.

No John-a-Dreams, no Laurence Olivier, no George Castille. It's not the mirror's reflection that kills us, on account of we ain't that kind of glass, children. We are not a mirror, but a diver's mask—a lens through which we look on inconsolable currents. Once we seen that, none of us wants to move. Nothing consoles us, and our longing drifts through the world, beyond it…even beyond the gods we imagine.

You are shredded by circumstance. Or you see everywhere the horror or absurdity of being. You drown like the crazy girl, or you understand:

Best never to be born. Next best, to die young.

Brischords: There is shredding and there is shredding. A term vague around the edges, rending asunder or the metal playing V-1 rocket dive on the whammy bar.

Falcon: The boy Vincent is bound for both. You seen his powers to charm and transform by shredding. Hella pretty, fingers cascading over the frets, the guitar between his legs like a ginormous strung pecker, pivoting, the neck high and standing as he slows into a walking "Voodoo Chile."

Daddy Chrome: All of this on the stage in the park, because early on that other one showed him the outlets, there for the lights and sound equipment. The stage gives Vincent freedom:

electrified, he can wail and embrace the volume, try music that shakes too many things at home, dream retro dreams of Eddie Van and Stevie Ray. And yes, the shredding stirred nerves up on the Court, but the LMPD lets it slide, too busy fighting their losing battle against Fourth and Fellini. Because they can't change the tide of things, and they know it.

DJ Mel: I come down from 4th and F the night that boy played, drawn by the groove. I told him I was *a personal friend of Bootsy Collins,* and I aks him if he knew who that was, and he says he made his funk the P-Funk, so I lingered a while, then went home to the bus stop and wig shop and C.V.S., but I swore I'd return the next time.

T. Tommy: We all was there the next time, Mel. Sat before the stage, in the orchestra rather than the seats. Give the boy a hand when he finished up that slow, serpentine blues improv and took it up to a flurry of quick, bending notes. It scared him at first, then, he bowed, but by then I was certain he would not forthcome with money.

So I warn him to keep an eye, and you all heard me and were in agreement. Keep an eye, I told him, on account of outdoor wiring—especially this wiring—is decrepit, capable of electrifying those who are not mindful.

He allowed he was fine, but thank you nonetheless.

Falcon: Brought up right and taught not to patronize.

DJ Mel: Safe enough to be polite, though, Falcon. Because he knowed he would never dress in worn lamé and sleep in a Goodwill box.

T. Tommy: Hey now, Mel. Keep an eye. My warning was genuine, and not for his donation. I emphasized the leaky stage structure, how everything it offered lay open to the elements, even those parts that should have been covered, and the boy thanked me again. Then I tell him it had happened to me before, on Halloween night in '68.

And he passed from amusement to interest, clean through alarm and out the other side of boredom.

Daddy Chrome: He expected otherwise. He had heard of the Lizard King, and when the story turned to you and the storm in the tower, he stopped believing, then stopped caring, then finally stopped listening, packed his guitar and took the amp downhill to the van…

Falcon: Which he parked right here, by the bench, by this rock-shattered streetlamp.

T. Tommy: Rock-shredded, children. Shredded with music and cast stones.

He did not hear the thing backstage. Because he wasn't listening, or it wasn't ready to be heard. But the three of you did, and if you didn't, I heard enough for you. That is why I told the story to all of you, to the stone lions and the empty stage and the blonde boy and the Brischords.

And I will tell it all again when the god arrives.

35. Stasimon: Antistrophe: Polymnia and the Muses

Polymnia: It may be the most popular of your plays. More than the harder ones about shredded families, unbalanced southern women, witch hunts, and dying salesmen. And still, not everyone gets out of *Our Town* alive. But death approaches dressed in homespun poetry, so it doesn't seem as much like death, but like a play about death.

Thalia: No sex either. No language that rankles the reverent. That is why Antioch likes *Our Town*.

Melpomene: Except the ghost. They do not like the ghost for religious reasons.

Thalia: Yes, that. *Hamlet* or *A Christmas Carol* or even *Casper* scents their nostrils with brimstone.

Polymnia: Peter Koenig rather likes *Our Town* in spite of everything. Especially the third act, which they rehearse tonight. Tell me how it goes, sisters.

Melpomene: It takes place twelve years after the first act. Begins in an abstract cemetery, set upon a hill overlooking Grover's Corners. About a dozen people sit in several rows of chairs, which are supposed to represent graves…

Thalia: Which solves all kinds of prop and staging problems. Stripped and minimal and high-school-drama artsy. Saves money on tombstones. The Stage Manager has been talking to the audience all along. Breaking the frame—artsy touch…

Oh those of you who listen here, who watch this drama from a silent place, we will not break the frame on you. We will speak in your imagined absence. But the Stage Manager, you were saying…

Melpomene: the Stage Manager tells us that these seated actors are the dead citizens of the town. A funeral procession approaches. The dead narrate the new arrival: Emily Webb, the play's romantic heroine, if you can call her that. She has died, it seems, while giving birth to her second child.

Her ghost walks away from the living and joins the dead, sitting next to Mrs. Gibbs, her mother-in-law.

Emily goes on and on about the world of the living, but she knows that world is behind her. That the dead are waiting for something.

Thalia: For over two millennia, I have adorned sarcophagi. I have looked back over processions in marble and stone and watched you erode as you follow. I could tell these dead how little they wait for, but I am only audience and dare not break the frame. But the dead are onto something when they detach from the troubles of the living.

Polymnia: Perhaps the last thing they are onto. I do not know.

Melpomene: Mrs. Gibbs tells Emily to wait, that it is best to be quiet and patient, but she is not having any of it. She decides that you can return to the world of the living, revisit the past.

Thalia: Our artsy, folksy Stage Manager offers to help, for after all, he's not just a stage manager, he's a damned narrative device!

Melpomene: Over Mrs. Gibbs' protests, Emily returns to her 12th birthday, where Americans live most of their lives. But it seems that everything overwhelms her, that she's undone by all she took for granted. She chooses to go back to the numbing comfort of the grave, says goodbye to the world in a speech that always seems to bring people to tears, no matter how much it is contrived and engineered to squeeze out every sniffle and saline drop.

The world, poor dead Emily tells us, is too wonderful for anyone to understand: "Oh, earth, you're too wonderful for anyone to realize you. Do any human beings ever realize life while they're in it?—every, every minute?"

Thalia: Of course not, girl. If they did it would be unbearable. Oblivion soothes the nerves. Which may be why people love this play. Because at the end, the actors all decide that life was sad and happy at the same time, wonderful and bittersweet. And all together, the dead start to wean themselves away from life, getting the ol' cosmic perspective, I suppose.

Or *I reckon*, as the Stage Manager might say.

Melpomene: But at play's end, George, Emily's husband, returns to weep at her grave. And to him the dead condescend, as does the Stage Manager to all of us, telling us all to go home and get a good night's sleep.

Thalia: All a good show, small town family values and good old Middle Amurrica. Entertaining, even moving in a tame way. Though tonight it will go differently at Antioch. Tonight it will not be how the play turns out.

Polymnia: And no matter the performance, it is never how the dead let go.

Remember, daughters of Memory?

First they set our sarcophagus by the roadside. It was custom in northern Italy at the time. And we felt the weight and the lost heat of the body behind our procession, something in the dark beginning to simmer with decay and scavenging life. Fetor and liquescence, I am sure, but it is long past and now I remember only the boiling, the crackle of insect life and the slow, smokeless burning. Above all, the eddy of energy against the marble interiors, the old *animula vagula blandula*, the pale little wandering soul, or maybe just the body's last refusal. And the thing moved, slowly at first among the remains and along the inner walls of the sarcophagus, but then more urgently, battering the marble, its cries whistling like a wind out of nowhere as it whirled more quickly, more desperately, confined in a narrow space. Like a bird battering itself in panic against a cage, it buffeted against us...

Thalia: It startled me, because it was not supposed to end like this. I mourned for the *animula*, my smiling mask shaking in the relief of my hand...

Polymnia: ...while the rest of us listened—still, pale, embedded—

as the spirit eventually gave up, as its movement dwindled and stopped at last. None of this do you see in Grover's Corners or at Antioch, where Peter Koenig and at least two tiers of ministers and assistant ministers dance attendant on rehearsals. No wonder Our Town puts people in the seats. The death it shows you is bearable, clean and sculpted. It is the slow decline of autumn into a waiting for eternity, not a seething in narrow space that ends nowhere.

36. Episode: The Road to Antioch

Exeunt THE MUSES. Manet POLYMNIA.

They threaten him with leaving the production.

Stephen drums his fingers on his knee and looks across the table at the relentless twins. "This doesn't show much commitment on your part."

"Oh, but we think it does, Mr. Thorne," Vincent replies. "The play needs music. We need a driving bass line, and Jack Rausch is just the one to provide it."

"I have no objections to him," Stephen admits. "He seems like a good kid, with plenty of looks and charisma. We could even find him a role in the play, on those virtues alone. But I object to being arm-twisted by some kind of amateur actors' strike."

Maia leans back and narrows her eyes. But Vincent, ever soothing, speaks words of reconcilement until Stephen smiles, knowing he is being cajoled. The twins have plans: Stephen

167

himself will go with them to Antioch, providing the arguments and leverage to wrest Jack Rausch from his prison and onto the stage in the park.

Now, waiting in front of the gates to Peter Koenig's massive mega-temple, Stephen wonders who is guiding this rescue mission. He feels as though Vincent has handed the reins to him, as director and prince of the process. There will have to be, of course, a facing of Koenig himself, but Stephen is armed with enough dramatic knowledge and artistic outrage to confront that dragon. He is so convinced of his rightness that he has let Vincent's enigmatic statement—that Aron is arranging the rescue—go unheeded.

Then Vincent's Volkswagen Eurovan unloads in front of the church, and the heavy, lamé-clad article stepped forth, followed by an unlikely but familiar *thiasos* Stephen already knows as the Brischords—two mulleted white people and a black man resplendent in a corona of picked Afro—all in bulky androgynous clothing.

He found them in the park, Vincent claims. And they have offered their allegiance and services.

What that could possibly mean, Stephen can only wonder. The chorus is one thing, but he is nervous that the Brischords have entered the story earlier than planned. Tommy is in half-Elvis, a ratty, linen duster draped over the lamé. Effusive and witty in his conversation, he smells bad nonetheless, as do his companions— the predictable dried-fruit smell of winos—and they shear off as Stephen approaches the gates of Antioch, bound for somewhere down the fence line and vanishing into the shadows.

The gates to the back campus are open night and day, easily entered, but the Antioch complex was indeed complex, and soon Stephen loses his way among the buildings, the theatre out of sight behind the Youth Center, the Counseling Headquarters, the gym, and the food court. Stephen swears under his breath again, and wanders until he finds the long, near-empty parking lot of the church. Perhaps the twins just might be bringing him in to sweep up after their whim and drama.

His apprehension grew as he glimpses Dolores Starr's old Charade straddling two parking spaces, and Stephen recalls vaguely that she had known Koenig some time back.

It is 8 pm, and apparently one of the few weeknights when Antioch offers no evening service. At the door's resistance to his pull, Stephen snorts, then caught himself with the understanding that a place has the right to be locked now and then. Most of the cars are clustered around a rather large building beside and behind the church, so he headed there.

The sound of raised voices and bogus accents reaches him. He can tell a high-school cast, even when he barely overhears them. Stephen follows the intonations, and a last door opened into a lobby, a climate-controlled theatre with cushioned and tiered seating, expensive and subtle lighting, and an enviable sound system. He settles into the back row, considerably behind four young men whose hair is quasi-long and stylishly sculptured, all of whom whisper idly and pretend to watch *Our Town*, which, as best Stephen remembers, is ending its second act up on the stage.

As the Stage Manager and Mrs. Soames exchange their platitudes of uncertainty and praise about the institution of marriage, Dolores Starr moves surprisingly into the seat beside Stephen. She laughs softly at his expression, whispered that she had brought Aron here *to rescue Jack Rausch*, stares down one of the young men who had turned around to shush her, then gracefully fields the solicitous *may we help you?* from another.

Stephen grins, links his fingers behind his head, and leans back in the suddenly comfortable seat. Now he enjoys the luxury of it all, and as the lights go up between the acts and the hands set a dozen or so chairs in a row to limn the cemetery, he catches himself remembering, after a long intermission, some of the things he liked about Dolores Starr.

"No, I have no idea," she replies to Stephen's questions about where his actors had gone. "I do know there's a plan to spring Jack Rausch free from this Baptist Thornton Wildlife preserve. It's almost good theatre, if you think about it. Here we are, hanging on the third act, witness to a play where we know the ending, but…"

"But that play is not the real play tonight, is it?" Stephen asks, squinting toward the bare stage for unexpected movement in the wings.

"Don't interrupt, Stephen. Even if you're right. Because it isn't the real play, we know that, but we aren't sure what's around and behind it. We can guess where things might end up and hope for something more interesting than we expected, even though we are usually disappointed."

Stephen turns to her. "Sorry."

"Oh, Stephen. You didn't actually think I meant you by that, did you?"

"No. Sorry for interrupting." His gaze turns back to the stage, and he masks a faint smile, convinced he has called her out. Such little dramas are as entertaining as anything Antioch might produce. No doubt he would have waited for the next thing with amusement and pleasant suspense, but Dolores drops the news.

George Castille, it seemed, is on the premises.

37.Episode: Leaving Our Town

Polymnia: Enter the first of the dead, taking their places behind the chairs on stage, muttering, exchanging jokes, two of the departed in amiable teenaged roughhouse. Awaiting the beginning of the scene, when they will spring into borrowed life, exaggerated gestures and estimated British accents. Some will be disguised as the elderly when their time comes, but these are early rehearsals—no costume, no makeup, no dramatic bend-over—so it is impossible to tell some of the principals—Mrs. Gibbs, Mrs. Soames—from the anonymous cloud of witnesses surrounding them.

Stephen again leans back in the unfairly comfortable chair. "Never seen so many teenagers side by side in a graveyard," he whispers. "Was there one of those high-school rampage killings at Grover's Corners?"

Dolores stifles a cry, slaps his shoulder playfully. "You are *still* the worst, Stephen!"

He smiles, then burst out laughing as she leaned toward

171

him and whispered.

"Yep, Grover's Corners is changin'. Them new-fangled metal detectors. Them assault rifles."

One of the ardent youth ministers shushed them, until Dolores stared him down again.

She swears she had no idea what Aron was planning, and seems troubled when Stephen told her about Vincent and the new staff of vagrants. As the Stage Manager sets the scene, pointing out all the vistas from the imaginary hilltop cemetery, one of the ministers slips out, smiling and nodding nervously at Stephen and Dolores as he scurries up the aisle.

The Stage Manager is dispensing folksy wisdom. How we all know that *something* was eternal. Is way down deep in every human being.

"I expect we'll be evicted soon," Dolores predicts. "That friendly nod wasn't friendly. Hope whatever Aron's planning is underway by now."

Stephen shrugs. "Maybe he's gone to get Koenig. As I recall, you were a favorite back in the day."

Dolores stiffens, and for a moment he thought she had taken offense again. Then he follows her gaze to the stage.

Where Tommy and the Brischords—mulleted, afro-picked, and stretched in lamé—have settled among the back row of chairs, intoning the almost choral observations of the dead.

About the funeral, they speak. About Emily Webb Gibbs, the heroine, who has just died in childbirth.

And then Maia De Chevre joins their number as the Emily in question.

She began all that long exchange with "Mother Gibbs" about how the living had no idea, how the world she was leaving was so beautiful, and Stephen leans forward, gaping, wondering aloud to Dolores why nobody has told him Maia was in this play.

He caught a whiff of something stronger than wine. The

astringent tug of juniper.

How much these days?

"Oh, she isn't, Stephen," Dolores replies. "The De Chevres are Catholic. They'd smile at her here, but hardly cast her. Maia made fun of the play when we did it at the high school, but she made a passable Emily, I thought."

"And she's passing again," Stephen observes.

Together they watch the third act flow toward those moments when Emily's ghost leaves the cemetery and descends through terrain and time to the Grover's Corners of her twelfth birthday years before, into a poignant brightness and intensity in which every lived moment gathers weight by associations, by perspective and loss. And even though both of them loathe the play, again they are caught by its ability to press each convergence of nerve and vessel.

"Damn it if it doesn't still get to me, Dolores," Stephen whispers, and she murmurs assent. We could imagine them sitting here until the Stage Manager tells them to go home, but the reverie breaks at Mrs. Webb's bustling, excessive entrance— the mother poor insubstantial Emily had returned to visit in vain.

For the mother is George Castille in apron and bouffant wig, gesturing in his most persuasive impersonation of Jessica Tandy. He and Maia play the scene off one another with a kind of mother-daughter chemistry, Maia with a strange, subdued passion that brings forth an unexpected fatherly instinct in Stephen Thorne, while George twists an exaggerated maternal instinct into a skewed sense of comedy, like Medea played by a drag queen. The other two ministers rise and leave with a rush, the clamor of their voices fading through the lobby. They return within minutes, as the play moves toward the last contrivance, when Emily's husband, George Gibbs—played by Vincent De Chevre—rushes onto the stage and falls grieving onto the grave.

They have done it, Stephen marvels: his little cast has hijacked the staple of American theatre and done so impressively, translating the reflexes of the play into something sharp and disruptive, distorting the poetry in all of its mawkishness into fireworks exploding over wearied ground.

But he is damned if he knows *why* they have done it.

"That's Peter in the hall," Dolores whispers nervously. Stephen lays a hand reassuringly on her shoulder, allowing with a smirk and bravado that whatever the charges—from criminal trespass to kidnapping—he will shoulder them for all.

Nor did his courage fail him when they emerge into the lobby to the angry glare of Antioch's entire youth ministry staff, while behind them, taller by a head than the loftiest assistant pastor, Peter Koenig regards them with puzzlement, exasperation, and a hint of amusement.

Behind this encounter of principals, Aron Starr hustles the Rausch boy into Dolores' Charade, Jack casting one last look toward the theatre as the tinted windows on the auto's passenger side close to obscure whatever thought or movement will pass between the boys on the way to their destination.

They are like athletes, their contest either over or ready to begin.

As Peter and Stephen turn to face each other in complete incomprehension.

But no more so than the incomprehension of Aron Starr, driving his mother's old Charade north up the interstate and regarding the mystery in the passenger's seat beside him.

Jack has come willingly, as though being yanked from the stage in mid-rehearsal was a matter of course. Now he rides where Aron takes him, passive but alert, watching the reflection of streetlights as it rushes across the windshield of the speeding car.

`"Dude," Aron begins, and Jack smiles, leaning forward a little in the seat. "Dude, there's something we haven't planned for in this."

Jack laughs softly. "Oh, *really*! Which is…?"

"So, where are you going to stay, Jack? I can take you across the bridge to Jeffersonville. Where is it that your family lives over there?"

"Oh, I don't believe I should go back there, Aron," Jack replies, leaving the options hanging.

"So. Then...I been thinking, Jack. Maybe you oughta stay at Mr. Thorne's or Mr. Castille's. You'd probably prefer Mr. Castille's, I'm guessing?"

To which Jack, "I bet neither of them knows you're planning their house guests. They'd both probably freak at the prospect, so no, that's out of the question."

"Are you having second thoughts, Jack?"

"Just saying that neither Mr. Thorne nor Mr. Castille would be expecting me. And why would I 'prefer Mr. Castille'?"

Aron pauses, glared uncomfortably out at the road. "I was just thinking, I suppose."

"'Thinking'? 'Supposed'?"

"You kinda struck me as being more comfortable at Mr. Castille's. Your hair. And...you and Vinnie. Right?"

Jack yawns and stretches slowly in the cramped car seat. "As you said, I'm just springing free of Antioch for a while. Thanks for getting me out of there. School's out, so I don't have to go back there. And only my grandmother will notice I'm missing at home. I can stay around here. In the city. Help on your play instead of *Our Town*. You need music for *The Bacchae*, I think?"

They drive on in what Aron takes to be perplexed silence. Jack produces an IPod, starts to put on the earphones. Aron takes them swiftly past the airport and the UPS terminal, his thoughts scrambling as he considers what to do with the passenger, if only where to lodge him for the night.

"So, Jack? What's Antioch like?"

Jack takes out one of the phones and regards his driver. "A church, Aron. Just your regular church, except it's enormous. Pretty respectable, everyone up to good clean fun, which they don't really see is too clean to be fun. Koenig's all right. The assistant ministers are mostly dicks, but that's the way it is most anywhere, right? The little guys jockey for power, and the big guy's got nothing to prove. Maybe they're dicks so Reverend Koenig doesn't have to be…"

The car slows in more congested traffic by the old Fairgrounds. Up ahead you can see the blue flashing lights of a police cruiser, sorting out a minor collision that has strung out the traffic for a couple of miles. Aron decides to take the exit near his home, to go surface roads and drop Jack off where Jack needs dropping off, in someone else's home and away from this slow, channeled movement of traffic. He knows his mother would have preferred a more conventional way of getting Jack away from Antioch, but their plan had seemed so awesome at the time, so filled with meta-possibility. He thinks Dolores will come around, will actually begin to relish this bold abduction. The De Chevres, after all, think she is amazing, think she was the mom everyone wanted to have. He had seen her standing with Mr. Thorne and Reverend Koenig as he and Jack made their break for the car.

She had dated them both, back in the day. He wonders why neither of them worked out for her. Maybe it was the drinking, or maybe something else. Whatever the case, he was vaguely glad they hadn't.

"So, Jack? You and Koenig? He's pretty cool, you say? Does he like you? I mean, do you guys get along and stuff? I know, it's none of my—"

Jack waves his hand sinuously. "I know…my hair, right? Naw, even if, Koenig's straight, man. And hey, just because you hear about them ministers with meth-head hustlers and wide stances in airport men's rooms…well, that don't mean there's a course on that in seminary, you know. Most of them are pretty mainstream dudes, even the prick assistant ministers. And you know, after all…"

"What?"

"Never mind, Aron."

"No…what?"

"I'm just going be around for the play, dude. I don't want to put anybody out. We can find me a couch somewhere to crash,

I guess. So if it's not Mr. Thorne's place or Mr. Castille's—and we both know it *so* shouldn't be either of them—maybe I can put up at the De Chevres' a while. After all, Vinnie and Maia both wanted me in the neighborhood."

Jack grins and puts on the earphones, and suddenly Aron's imagination reels with the possibility that he had it wrong, had miscalculated the whole venture. His hope, manufactured on the park stage earlier in the week, that the conversation between Jack and Maia was simply something between friends, that her hand on the other boy's shoulder was a sign of solidarity, of alliance, suddenly begins to dismantle. After all, he hadn't heard what they were saying, had just stood there probably looking dumb and lumpish while a beautiful pair talked and laughed and perhaps confided…

The idea of Jack Rausch under Maia's roof. Aron's imagination fails: he cannot piece together what the DeChevre place looks like. He has never been invited. And without set and backdrop, sultry scenes became more possible.

A bedroom. White smooth sheets. The commingling of skin, fair and dark…

A blind surge passes over Aron Star, and for a moment he glimpses a hot glade, a hallucinatory darkness, something picking him up and carrying him and dropping him…

He speaks Jack's name aloud twice. Then the third time, hearing him at last, the boy removes the earphones entirely. "Yes, Aron?"

"We can try Mr. Thorne's place first. Failing that, I guess my mother wouldn't mind if you stayed at our place a little while."

"How hospitable, Lord Dionysus. I guess you're not the bad host everybody claims."

Only Jack's riddling smile suggests that Aron's new lodger was teasing.

38. Episode: Where Are You Going?

Enter T. TOMMY BRISCOE, who stands center stage beside POLYMNIA.

Polymnia: Maia looks out the window of the family Eurovan onto the corner of Fourth and Fellini.

As Vincent steered off the St. Catherine exit, she had tried to lock the doors inconspicuously, without ruffling the attentions or the feelings of the passengers. Mel B and Daddy Chrome are whispering in some wine-ignited contradiction across Falcon, who sits between them, sullenly silent since Vinnie has asked her not to smoke in the van. Nevertheless, the vehicle smells of stale tobacco, stale wine, and stale bodies, and Maia wants her brother's new friends let off by the laundromat rather than taken all the way to the dodgy intersection.

T. Tommy has kept silent until now. Seated farthest back, alone in the third row of seats, he begins to speak as they cross Second Street and approach Third, the Walnut Street Baptist Church on their left.

Tommy: This is your granddaddy of the mega-church, Gemini. Third and St. Catherine, called Walnut Street Church in commemoration of where it begun, north of Broadway in another locale entirely. Telecasts since television, services packed until the 'sixties when half the white people moved east. Now they come here defensively, their doors all locked on the way to Jesus.

Polymnia: Maia's hand moved from the door to her lap. She bites her lip and blushes in the dark as the streetlight spills across the passengers.

Tommy: People don't know, children, about the bell in yonder church. How it was donated as the twentieth century turned by a man who gave the money on the assurance that no black folks would ever worship there. Walnut Street—the street, not the church—goes by Muhammad Ali Boulevard now, in honor of the fighter. Would it be ironic, you think, if a mosque was to someday take over this site, make this Constantinople into Istanbul?

Polymnia: The van turns left, headed past the abandoned Winn-Dixie and the row of dollar stores, wig shops, and the one decent Chinese takeout in the city.

Tommy: Someone bought up half this block years back. For development, mind you. But the LMPD will tell you it's a place where crack deals conspire. There is dark history interconnected here. I dare say no more. Now, if you'd let us off at the corner, young Vincent. I am pleased we could help you be insubordinate, but now it is back to work as the abandoned we go.

Polymnia: "We won't abandon you," Vincent insists. "You've made some friends here, T. Tommy."

Tommy: Oh, isn't that good to know, young Vincent. And you've visited Antioch as a kind of bonus. Things are large there, I know. And not quite earnest, I'm guessing.

There is the drug store at the threshold of which I saw two Jehovah's Witnesses saving a drag queen who had stopped in full regalia for a bottle of Gordon's and a carton of Vogue Menthols. She was weeping when the spirit settled, and I have heard that she indeed adopted the name Grace Descending in later appearances with the girls at Flaming 'Mo's.

And there is the crossing light, where the Sign-Talking Brother comes when hallucinogens are on him. Disco survivor, copper thief, gas money negotiator by day, by night he comes to the corner, as he will shortly, children. And here he holds forth against the white and glowing walking man before the red hand of God rises to compel his silence."

Polymnia: "It ain't everyone that bad off on the corner, am I right, Tommy?" Vincent asks.

Tommy: Don't say 'ain't', son. It is beneath your stature. But you are otherwise right in part, because there is Bus Stop Jesus, who begs for cigarettes a block north by the Methodist Church, then blows kisses at passing cars. He's showing four paintings in a gallery on Main Street and sleeping behind the hundred-dollar steakhouse less than a block from his exhibit. So is he not so bad off, or is he worse because the door he can't open is ajar for him, and they is light on the other side?

We'll embark here, children. Lock your doors and don't say 'ain't'. And may the peace of the Lord that passeth all understanding keep your hearts and minds…"

(Exit TOMMY)

Polymnia: And T. Tommy makes the sign of the Cross over the children, and he and the Brischords labor off into the baffled night. Vincent dutifully locks the doors behind them, and an approaching beggar turns disconsolately away.

Ahead the lights are out in the Chinese restaurant, and at the corner opposite, the Sign-Talking Brother approaches the intersection through the back lot of the boarded bank, already speaking in angry tongues.

"We'd better be going, Maia," Vincent urges, turning west onto Oak toward the Ninth Street intersection and the road to home and safety.

And Maia looks through the glass at a gaunt black woman, curled fetally under the CVS sign, eyes unfocused and yellowed by the pipe. For a moment they lock gazes, and with something resembling recognition Maia sees the youth in the woman, sees her laughing with church friends and aspiring to nursing school. Maia realizes the woman is not much older, not really, and for a moment her heart turns that way, met mid-glance by the woman's vacant eyes. And the woman sees the blonde girl's face in the window of the van, marking her and marking the vehicle, and knowing that the time is coming when the van doors will open.

39. Jack O' Dreams

Polymnia: Never one to give up the first plan right away, the strange enthusiasm of an hour before having ebbed, left at the wheel with his drowsing passenger, Aron brings Jack to Stephen Thorne's doorstep. There they find Thorne, George Castille, a fifth of scotch and an acrid, nutty smell in the room, though Stephen hastens to open the window at their arrival.

Stephen plays the cool old hippie, announces that he disapproves of the recent abduction but loves how they all had gone about it. Behind Stephen, Castille winks conspiratorially at the boys, then tells them that since they are here, Mr. Thorne has announcements regarding the casting of the play.

Aron stiffens at the prospect of changes, but relaxes visibly when Stephen makes known his intentions to play old Cadmus himself, the grandfather of Dionysus and Pentheus, while Mr. Castille will play the ancient prophet Tireisias. *Our Town*, it seemed, has reminded the men how tedious it was to watch young and amateur actors play characters five times their age.

Relieved and emboldened that he is still Dionysus, still the star, Aron asks Stephen Thorne whether Jack can crash there *until things blow over at Antioch.*

The glance exchanged by Cadmus and Tireisias is one of horror. They were not about to follow the god's command, and both insist they had no room for guests. Neither mentions how awkward it might be for a grown man to house a seventeen-year-old boy who was neither his son nor relative, but it confirms what Aron had suspected, what he had talked about to Jack in the ride home from Antioch. So he concedes his mother might make the better host, that Jack might stay with them, if only briefly, and both men calms and return to planning the play, as Aron silently plans what to say to Dolores.

She lets Jack stay, of course. Something about being accustomed to cleaning up after men, after all their messes. So Aron stopped worrying about that part of it, set Jack up on the sofa.

Jack slept uneasily under Dolores Starr's roof, his thoughts disrupted by a strange but inevitable dream in which, to the sound of one of his own bass runs, the brick houses on Fourth Street trembled with a borrowed light, and unseasonable birds perched in the branches and wires along the avenue._

He controlled his dream and did not control it, both swept on and guided by the flow of a hot summer wind channeling down the street, stirring discarded paper cups and plastic bags into little cylclones whirling atop the sewer grates. Something in the city was rising, was casting aside accustomed order, and Jack smelled something turned and feral on the breeze.

Somewhere, in some imagined alley amid the old Victorian walking courts, a big cat was stretching its slow thighs and beginning to move inescapably toward the light of the theater and a destination lost in dreaming.

40. Episode: Annoying the Tao

Polymnia: You took him from sure success, from a supportive crowd, she says. You caused all kinds of trouble with a powerful, successful man, so that this boy can play music for your doomed production.

She isn't crazy for Peter Koenig either, she assures him, but he is a respectable man, and decent, and frankly, Stephen, this behavior is simply juvenile.

The coins have given him the fortieth hexagram. *Kieh.* Relief.

Have warned him that *the third SIX, divided, shows a porter with his burden, riding in a carriage. He will tempt robbers to attack him. However firm and correct he may try to be, there will be cause for regret.*

But then, in *the sixth SIX, divided, we see a feudal prince with his bow shooting at a falcon on the top of a high wall, and hitting it. The effect of his action will be in every way advantageous.*

He knows that Muriel would win the small arguments, as usual. That she will entangle him in her thickets. He also knows that winning the argument does not make her right. Her disapproval of Jack Rausch's abduction was justified; her reasons were not.

It was hardly kidnapping, he assures her. Jack is free to come and go as he pleases, not kneeling and hooded in some admonitory video, with some hulking, sword-brandishing Taliban above him. And after all, the boy had come willingly, had expressed no enthusiasm for yet another *Our Town*—a play so exhausted and over-produced that every amateur actor in the city has appeared in one version or another.

She allows this might be so, but reminds him that he once directed *The Crucible*, and everyone preferred a wholesome small town to a tired old Arthur Miller Salem witch hunt, complete with hysterical young people and ill-guided parsons. She was surprised, she suggests, that Stephen had not dressed the cast in contemporary clothing to imply the play was a commentary on the Bush Administration, and when Stephen asks her what on earth that was supposed to mean, she shifts ground again, this time sliding through bracken and undergrowth, asking him what plays he had directed at Yale, at Kent. Whether they might have included *Our Town*.

In (the state indicated by) Kieh advantage will be found in the south-west. If no (further) operations be called for, there will be good fortune in coming back (to the old conditions). If some operations be called for, there will be good fortune in the early conducting of them.

Get it over early, he tells himself. Muriel Thorne is enough to annoy the Tao out of you.

She isn't sure that she will attend the opening of Stephen's *Bacchae*. June is always so hot in Louisville, and after all, she has seen the play before. Even auditioned for the part of Agave, she reminds him.

He asks why she so liked seeing *Our Town* again and again.

She responds, enigmatically, that it is different.

Then Stephen asked if it is different because this *Bacchae* is *his Bacchae*, and she wonders how he can say such a thing, knowing that she lives and dies with his hopes and the disappointments that always follow. Like Yale. Like Kent. But recently, too.

It is why, she says, she had to leave his *Crucible* at the end of the first act, when Betty and Abigail made their list of those they had seen with the Devil. It was bad enough what Joe McCarthy had done to all those people, but Arthur Miller would not let it drop and had to rehearse it through these ridiculous Puritan girls. And to make matters worse, her own son had directed a version that Wade Abner had called *excruciblating*. In the ensuing weeks, when everyone had recovered, she had mustered the courage and maternal love to go through the photo stills from the performance. To even order a few prints of her own.

Stephen reminds her that she had ordered photos of one Muriel Thorne, seated in the front row of the theatre, hair hennaed and in slight overdress. Six of them, as he recalls. And none of anything else.

There is no need to scold, she replies, her voice wounded, briefly inaudible amid acoustic shadow, her voice rattling and dodging, then surging back in a chittering of static as though she had emerged from a cavern of bats. She has so few good photographs of herself, after all, and all of her friends were clamoring for one. In fact, she wishes now she had ordered more of them. They would have salvaged something from that horrible night.

He would hope dearly, Stephen says, that his own mother would reconsider. And then the answer rose from the hexagram, offered the escape.

If some operations be called for, there will be good fortune in the early conducting of them.

Perhaps we could make allowances for weather, Stephen offers: if the night of dress rehearsal promises to break cooler, Muriel would be able to attend, thereby avoiding the empty seats and humiliations and Wade Abners of the opening night. It was something that George Castille's mother would have done, had not her death ten years ago prevented her.

Muriel doubts that Amanda Wingfield Castille would have been supportive of a son like that.

41. Episode: Twin Speak for the Head

The famed intuition of twins begins in amniotic bonding. Sometimes, on rare and heartbreaking occasions, the bodies join, wedding flesh and bone and vital organs, and one devours the other.

But more often—quite often—the soul's interweaving shows in a shared private language, the parts of which fit together like the halves of a ring in an old comedy, when twins separated at birth link a coin or a signet in the last scene of the play and discover they were bound together all along, that they are lucky they didn't violate taboos when they wanted each other in the second act.

As they grow older and necessities draw them apart, they sometimes develop an intuition, an extra sense between them. This is the case with human twins, as parapsychology maintains. But also with divinity, with Apollo and Artemis. So, too, perhaps, Castor and Pollux. Helen and Clytemnestra, though in their cases one twin was divine, the other mortal, and it was more difficult, of course, for two such different natures to commune with intimacy. In all cases, something like a soul traces in the chromosomal pattern, in blood or ichor or a blending of the two, for the gods know what the gods know, but the insight is larger than mortal.

Cassandra is more than a complex. True prophecy on disbelieving ears, a girl resisting the god's advances and punished for her resistance, for chastity. The god Apollo approached her, the story goes, all golden and beautiful, all oracle and sunlight and promise, expecting the trade-off as entitlement, his gift of foreknowledge at the price of her love.

There is another part of the story. Like Maia De Chevre, Cassandra was a twin. And when the festival was held to honor her birth and that of her brother Helenus, the two of them were put to bed in Apollo's temple, while parents and friends celebrated the occasion. Then, flushed with wine, the adults went home, forgetting the twins in the sanctuary. Next morning, sober again, they returned to the temple, where they found the sacred serpents coiled about the children, cleansing the infant eyes and ears with their flickering tongues. Frightened by the outcry of the woman, by the wail raised at this prodigious sight, the serpents disappeared among the laurel boughs which lay beside the infants on the floor. From that moment, it is said, Cassandra and Helenus possessed the gift of prophecy.

Cassandra and Helenus. She was cursed with others' disbelief, and prophesied the burning of a city to the laughter and doubt of its people, of her friends, her family. Meanwhile her brother supposedly prospered, touched by the god as well.

What did second sight tell him of her visions? He takes a place of prophetic honor among his people, though in some versions of the story he helps in their betrayal, even introduces the idea of the Trojan Horse to the Greeks. In all versions of the story, he survives.

But traitor or not, why does Helenus never defend his sister? Prophet himself, why does he never see she is right?

Another set of twins. Another time and city. Another

venue sacred to another god, a serpent coiled in its wings and recesses. So Maia, driving the hippie van to pick up her brother in the park, feels a stir in the energies and an unusual foreboding. But indeed, Vinnie De Chevre is quite content and peaceful, tuning his guitar for a first duet with Jack Rausch.

At home Aron sulks until Dolores said enough, they should get out for a while. He drives Jack into town, where Jack and Vinnie play music at the park, and Aron again sulks as the sun sets and the daylight tumbles into the first warm night of the season.

It is marvelous, he has to allow: Jack setting up a gamic, driving base, Vincent's batrachian lead climbing the line like a great, predatory snake, twining until it was enough to make a wino blush. And indeed T. Tommy's face is flushed, incandescent, as he and the Brischords emerge from the shadow, and take up a wailing, improvised call and response.

Then it begins, vines breaking the surfaces of treated wood, vegetating and burgeoning, the sets suddenly sprouting ivy and all of them playing, rapt by the music and indifferent to the dark greenery that encircled them. Aron alone, unmusical and seated on the topmost tier of the amphitheater, watches as all of it— players and singers, instruments, folly towers and mirrors—fall ambiguous and green.

It unnerves him, but he blames it on the light and the superlative weed the boys had nicked from a sandwich bag under Stephen Thorne's copy of *The Bacchae*, slipped there hastily and half-assed at the arrival of young and impressionable guests. And from where he sits, he could not see us dancing in the mirrors, our hair untied and disheveled, masked and wreathed, Thalia bearing a wine pitcher called the *oinochoe*. Now the music drives into an ambling, nasty medley of Elvis songs, as *Elvis* becomes *lives* and *evils* in the hands of raucously stoned musicians, lifting the songs out of the cleanly, castrated appeal of the Colonel Tom Parker years and giving funk and cojones to 'Viva Las Vegas,' 'Blue Moon of Kentucky', T. Tommy's glitter barely visible under the shadowy green as he rises to a solo 'Are You Lonesome Tonight' with the Brischords in a welling intoned background so lonely that Aron finds it the saddest sound he believes he has ever heard, like kissing a long-lost love through cold glass.

He breathes more easily when the music lifts up and away from him, buoyed on a dark warm wind and accompanied by a strange, desolate melody that the boy cannot recognize but was played offstage by a veiled Euterpe, sad on the double reeds of an *aulos*. Something like a *qeej* but sacred to the approaching god.

And the sound of the ancient flute lifts up and north over a stand of oak, past the sidewalk silvered in moonlight and north toward Ormsby and Oak Street beyond it, the infamous corner where the Brother talks to the crossing signs and where money and substances change hands in open streetlight, where the gaunt girl there only the night before has vanished, snatched off by the god that is both Dionysus and Hades and leaving a scarcely noticed emptiness amid the commerce and squalor—an emptiness the music did its best to fill.

And there, doors locked against intruders and night and melancholy wind, Maia De Chevre sits behind the wheel of the van and listens.

As far away from her, left backstage and overlooked in the ecstasy of rising music, the scaled god tremors and stretches.

42. Stasimon: Strophe: Polymnia and the Muses

Enter THE MUSES, who encircle POLYMNIA and begin to dance.

Polymnia: Sister ours, Lady of the Blood Moon. Virgin of the Nets. Artemis, shadow to your brother's light. Be near us as this story unfolds. As light and shadow meet this evening in Antioch, as Stephen Thorne meets with the Reverend Koenig in secret wrangling.

Thalia: You witness the foolery of men, Artemis Keladeinos. You call it foolery, as indeed it should be called, and yet…You know it is not only a pissing contest, not only a measurement of members…

For though size matters, not *that* size nor *those* matters…

You know their vanities, Sister, how they trump up the opposition.

How Stephen Thorne mimics the sonorities of Peter Koenig in his mind, mocks a voice accustomed to no challenge.

Melpomene: How Koenig, under a smile and false solicitude, is wondering why amateur directors see no difference between pretend and pretense.

How Peter Koenig is content that the Bible will endure when Euripides is ashes…

Thalia: How Stephen Thorne responds that Thornton Wilder is no Bible, much less Euripides, and that those who prefer the Bible to the tragedies have read neither one. As Stephen imagines *aw shucks* is neither ethics nor aesthetics…

Melpomene: Peter Koenig sees no art in obscurity or offense. As Stephen will not build up people falsely…

Thalia: Koenig will not tear them down for no reason.

Polymnia: All struggles are for power, and not all power is the same.

Melpomene: As Koenig expresses polite disapproval at Jack Rausch's abduction…

Thalia: while Stephen celebrates politely the boy's liberation,

Polymnia: it all comes back to blood and the letting of blood, to the hunt upon primal hillsides, where a man's will falls down below thought and language, coiling and seething until the cracks in the fissure, the oblique eruptions widen, reminding him briefly of the feral thing he is.

43. Stasimon: Antistrophe: T. Tommy and the Brischords

(TOMMY and THE BRISCHORDS enter from the orchestra. POLYMNIA and THE MUSES move stage right.)

T. Tommy: That night, barely twenty and a student at the university, I went to see the Doors at Freedom Hall.

The god was subdued that night, children. Baggy white jeans and a t-shirt, no bombast of tight leather. 'Hello, I Love You,' as his greeting, smoking and drunk evidently, theophany five days before the election that brought Nixon in, and something in history gone bad that you could smell under the cannabis.

I dropped the acid on the way home, thunderstorm rumbling out of the west. The last of the trick-or-treaters still on the street, the big kids, cheap masks and gerrymandered costumes—they were too old, had outstayed the holiday's welcome. And Nixon masks among them, as I tried to stay outside the trip while driving. By the time I reached campus I was sure the Republican Party was out to get me, and of course the acid, as always, was prophetic.

All the buildings were closed down and locked for the night, and I rode the fear like someone in a bad Hunter Thompson story until I found a door ajar in Gottschalk Hall, where someone had propped it open and forgot, so I slipped in out of the rising storm.

There is a small seminar room on the third floor. I knew it because I'd had a Moderns class there—Pound and Eliot, Joyce and Faulkner—believe me or don't, but I took the class and got a C+. There was a stairway off the room, and you could get to the roof, though it was unwise, they cautioned. And though it was unwise, I got there, and I looked out across the campus by night, through the trees toward the parkway and the old Confederate Monument.

And the bolt struck, and I felt it before I heared it, children, wild light and the top of my head sheared away and it was like my soles were soldered to the ground in sheer electric energy. For a moment I gained balance, and the branches opened and I saw city lights steady in a current of blackness, a current that broke across them and almost carried me with it, in rain and shadow, but I held my ground.

It took me a year to grow hair back. I was magnetized, could not wear a watch. I would black out and awaken at the overlook, sometimes naked, sometimes wrapped only in a blanket against imagined winds. And from then on I was asking Alice, drawn back like something primeval and tidal.

44. Stasimon: Strophe: Polymnia and the Muses

TOMMY and THE BRISCHORDS mount the stage, moving upstage left. POLYMNIA and THE MUSES move center stage.

Polymnia: Over here, Tommy. Down Fourth Street close and littered, then a block east past the fading statue for the Confederate Dead, to this place where we now sit sheltered and illumined. This museum, across from the krater, the wine vessel, on which the god appears, reclining in black-figure.

All these things I tell you are close in place and time. The god arrives on a stage of nine city blocks. Seven, if you don't count the side streets that branch to nothing off the main thoroughfares. Seen from above, the streets are hexagrams, and the lines change yin to yang, but mostly yang to yin, as the landscape settles, as ELIVS fades from sight and the god appears in dark radiance, changing the third line of the hexagram so that it no longer reads

197

Sovereignty but now Contradiction, as the King devolves into fragments.

Erato: Desire and power and love are elusive, all of the same until they sprout in fertile ground. But courtship is what the earth yearns for. A longing that is simple, terrible, to be vitalized. And in this desire, T. Tommy is no fool. He knows that divine invasion shapes receptive country and is shaped by it, but what that means is you keep calling on the god until you get the coiled thing backstage, something you half-expect at best.

Thalia: For example, sisters: the congregation at Antioch—those who yearn for the Rapture at least—would shit themselves at the form Apocalypse would take. Because the pleasure of imagining hell for their business rivals and political opponents would be short-lived. It would not pan out the way their malice has it plotted.

Melpomene: And if Aron Starr had come to life in the way Dolores imagines, those nights she stands above his sullen and nightstruck bed, this story would not end as she foresees.
    Not that it will, anyway.

Erato: Because what the passive earth takes in is transformed by its yielding soil. Forgotten seeds spring surprisingly to life, while others, mindfully planted and tended, sprout pale and grotesquely shaped by a week of unforeseen rain, by a passage of shadow or unseasonable cold snap.

Clio: And far from the earth, when hardened and fired, slipped or glazed to be hidden for centuries or housed in a well-lit museum, the clay still harbors life, the vessel commingles with what it contains, producing something that is neither or both. And *both* is *neither* in this game of divine *kottabos*, when the wine tossed by the god rings against the surface of the krater.
    In the week after Dolores looks down on her sleeping son,

the krater begins to change.

Erato: I saw it first and told them, Thalia and Polymnia. How Ariadne…

Thalia: …or the maenad—because we did not know who the girl was on the vase...

Erato: …or the maenad, then…had begun to change. She was aging now, her dark hair flecked with strands of gold that the experts would mark as wear on the surface of the krater rather than the woman's transformation.

Thalia: It was Dolores, aged and inebrious, staring across at the god. Or becoming Dolores, as fleshly and lost, somewhere she wandered through classes and rehearsals, the moving world around her becoming foggy and abstract, while Python's brush lines sharpened after two millennia of rest, gaining texture and layering over the clay.

We laughed at first, but we knew what the changes meant. Now the surface of the vessel shimmered and the steady museum light fluttered as it did only in passing storms.

Melpomene: And since I know the god best, I can tell you. He was filling the calyx, was nectar in the bud of the flower, blood in the ceramic heart that slowly, unavoidably, was starting to beat.

45. Episode: Rescued Again

(Exeunt TOMMY and THE BRISCHORDS. Manent POLYMNIA and THE MUSES)

Thalia: Aron shakes the dice in his hand. Trapped in a labyrinth of his own devising, now he is fastened to Jack Rausch. What had begun as courageous rescue has settled into an irritating daily life, his private schedule disrupted by company, his friends' allegiance as shifting as his mother's. He and Jack umbilically nourished at the same residence, but the guest more favored than the son.

Aron is being shredded by women. Or so he figures. For when he watches Maia's averted glance, how she brushes back her hair in a way she never had when visiting before, how the top button of her blouse is free, the collar framing the heartbreaking hollow of her throat…

Compromised by infatuations, Aron has sealed off the world of his game from Jack's entry. But tonight he rolls the dice and weaves scenarios for half an hour until he sensed impatience in the players, the restlessness of Vincent and Apache while Billy hovers at the refrigerator and Maia sits with Jack in the common room of the apartment.

So does nobody want to play or what? Aron asks into the lulled mood. And it is Vincent, ever the peace maker, who draws him aside at last, outside for cigarettes and advice, as he explains how all the others want Jack to rejoin the game.

Very well, Aron concedes. Because how might he do otherwise and not appear spiteful, mean, adolescent? But Jack has to earn his way back in. For after all, it is a game, isn't it? And the idea of a game—of *this* game, at least—is to test the wits of the players.

Polymnia: Often an RPG comes down to ingenuity. To simple dice roll and problem solving. Sometimes the whole *RP* in *RPG* dwindles even further, into cleverness and luck.

But surely there are those moments when the player becomes actor, is filled with the breath of the god and is transformed. Sometimes, even in those games where a single player acts as more than one character, the moment comes as he tumbles with assurance into one role, or the other, or even both—often in sequence or sometimes even simultaneously. *Enthusiasm,* George Castille called it: where the god fills the player. The moments the actor relishes, but also the reader, the story's listener, who finds himself in residence, translated to the world made of those words and gestures (or of those dice and maps and diagrams). A world that takes on shimmering life, like the way a constellation becomes a lynx, a dragon, a cup, when our eyes summon shapes from the spaces between stars.

Now Aron sets a maze before his players, yet another obstacle to the subterranean descent of Brendan and Melusine, Hrothgar and Kleptos. From the outside, it is simply five young people seated around a table. Vincent draws the others back to the game, including Jack, who stands behind Maia's chair, his hands on its high back.

But something is forming in the spaces between them. Perhaps only my sisters and I see it clearly.

Aron announces that the party of adventurers has found the body of a female cleric, sealed in a sleep resembling death, encased in impermeable crystal. His eyes meet Jack's as he tells them this.

Jack receives the reluctant gift with faint smiles and a nod, and quietly takes a seat at the table between the De Chevre twins.

Aron masks the dice roll and explains. *Surely there is some way to open the crystal casket. Surely something can revitalize the sleeping girl.*

Urania: It is now that I descend upon the little community. For though my sisters are almost all verbal creatures—muses of drama and poetry, history, epic, even dance—I am different. The stars I govern are stationary and abstract until drawn together by seeing and imagining. Because the heart cannot bear an unstoried world. And so the players in a game like this conjure flesh and nerve and place and journey from numbers and the chance roll of *astragali* and *tesserae*.

Polymnia: Billy Shepherd's shadow hulks on the wall, enlarging, assuming a bearish and bristling shape. No trick of the light except my sister Urania's starlight, in which Apache Downs' shadow dwindles, becoming slim and dexterous and febrile. In the mirrors of the Starr apartment, then, you can see fighters, a magic-user, a thief, and a golden girl in white robes, asleep in a crystal casing.

Aron casts no shadow. At best he leaves a ripple in the aether, something undetectable except for a voice that overlies the scenes in the mirrors, a quality of light that defines the shadows, hardens their edges.

The girl stirs in the cabinet, Aron intones. *Stirs in airless glass.*

And indeed, the priestess stirs, the thief crouches beside

her, desperately searching for seams in the faceted casket. Sister Urania is joined by Sister Thalia, who rises from the interstices of starlight and leans close to Apache Downs, whispering inspirations he is too thick to gather. Hrothgar and Brendan stood guard over the fiasco.

Thalia: Then the players' own muse, the flesh-and-mortal Maia, breathes clemency into Aron's improvised storm.

I lean over the casket, she announces. *I kiss the mouth of the priestess through the thin barrier of glass. For I know the old tales, wherein a kiss revives and restores the sleeping maiden.*

It takes no muse to see defeat settle upon Aron's shoulders like a grim and monitory bird, as, keeping with the roleplay but following the prompt of her rising desire, Maia De Chevre mouths a kiss less than an inch from Jack's parted lips, and the whole room tilted with a sharp intake of our breaths.

46. Episode: Unclear Jealousies

Thalia: Maia finally tells her brother that Jack had visited. Had dropped by the house a time last week after his school. That he had claimed he was looking for Vincent.

Jack had helped her lift some boxes to the attic, had labored under her teasing. Perhaps he should grow his hair like Samson, he offered, but Maia teased him, saying it would make him prettier, hardly stronger. They pushed and scuffled, both feigning wrath and tamping laughter. Erato's hand on Vincent's shoulder as Maia tells her brother how the pushes became gentler and more bodily, slipped into a slow wrangling of thighs and chests. How Jack and Maia slid to the attic floor, startled, still pretending at wrestling, raising dust amid De Chevre castoffs.

And when Vincent shivers an intake of breath and stares at his sister raptly, asking what came next, she turned and blushed, because of course *she* had come next, her gaze languidly, blissfully sinking into Jack's dark eyes as she lay back amid boxes and portmanteaux, dumbfounded and sexcellent, his slim bassist's fingers tracing patterns on her lower lip as she slipped his index finger under her tongue unto the first knuckle, looking up at him with drowsy, knowing eyes.

It is enough for her brother to hear this. Near breathless himself at Maia's account, reddening when she spoke of Jack's fingers, Vincent forbids his sister to be alone with the boy. Then at once recants. He is a better brother than counselor, after all, sitting on the De Chevre patio, smoking a stolen cigarette and trying to tell himself what he cannot tell himself.

We Muses watch as well, are exultant. Seeing possibilities and permutations in all of this, loving the sheer geometry of the scandalous triangle. Such events make inevitable motions, are lines converging in the distance. It takes no prophet now to see things ending badly.

47. Episode: Agon at Antioch

Polymnia: Roy Rausch belabors all things to Peter Koenig, two kings in uneasy counsel. And here, adding a third party—this party, especially, Dolores Starr—the air becomes volatile and male plumage is put to display. Rausch is still on about Jack's imagined deviance: inevitable, he supposes, among theatre people, ordained by the whereabouts of George Castille, and the primary sign of a fall from faith.

Peter faces the bluster from behind his desk, aware of Christ Equestrian (or Asinarian?) in the print behind him, knowing how Jesus must have felt, straddling a donkey's back.

The assemblyman stands at Dolores' arrival, does not shake hands, but nods according to the rules, as if to say he is polite to women even when the jury is out as to whether they are ladies. He asks Dolores whether it is true, whether Jack is staying with her and her son, and if he is, whether that is proper. When Dolores confirms Jack's presence and her own honorable intentions, Rausch settles back in his chair, steeples his fingers under his chin, and looked confidently at Koenig.

But Koenig cannot deliver. Or *will* not, imagining Jack better off sheltered in the fleshpots of Roy Rausch's imagining than on the streets like that chorus who had snatched him out of Grover's Corners. Koenig worries instead about the soul's migration, because there are things Jack Rausch needs that he cannot find in Antioch, and those needs are understandable and just.

Meanwhile, Roy takes up the outcry. He would take Dolores at her word. He says he knows that single mothers are often hard put to make the best of the consequences of their actions.

Thalia: And as she starts to speak, starts to crack the vessel and spill it all, the office door opens, admitting the formidable one-woman parade of Madeleine Rausch.

Dolores holds her counsel at the arrival of Jack's Maddaw.

Now the four of them array themselves like an epic debate, like a conclave of generals or demons, and instead of eloquence, when Maddaw asks for the whereabouts of her grandson, they all fall silent.

Melpomene: Roy Rausch looks to his mother and to the preacher, demanding simple answers to nuanced questions. Jack had always been intricate to love, and the assemblyman had ceased trying to do so on those mornings a dozen years ago, when the boy sat on Madeleine's lap looking at Roman images. Roy looked in on this intimate scene through the doorway, silent as a forgotten tutelary, wishing Jack had never returned there, wishing no ill on him but wishing he would just go away, watching as the two of them sat above Maddaw's photo album, harvesting sunlight and colors that, from his own vantage point, were blurred and indefinite and therefore menacing.

Peter Koenig is imagining as well. Trying to receive Madeleine Rausch with the dignity she expects, his thoughts veering nonetheless down a dark channel, he imagines the boy at the lean-to bus stop on the corner of 4th and Fellini, his dark hair matted by rain, his thin jacket clutched against hostility and the inclemency of a humid spring night. What could he have told Jack Rausch to keep and affirm him?

And Dolores meanwhile thinks of Aron, her ire at the assemblyman's jab against single motherhood sliding naturally toward concern for her own single child, lingering there briefly, then sliding away, as though she watches him through the door of a sunlit room. He was ousted and overwhelmed by Jack's gifts, by uncomplicated radiance, she concludes. The world wells in uncontrollable currents around them. In her mind's eye her son looks heavier, his eyelids pouched with 3 a.m. weariness, and she wonders again how he has betrayed his promise.

Madeleine Rausch is fed up with them all. She has arrived to jostle. At the source of local right-wing politics for fifty years, she knew that it all comes back to mirrors—mirrors like those Dolores had placed on stage at the theater. And though she will not be caught dead at any play of Stephen Thorne's—nor few at Antioch, for that matter—Madeleine Rausch sees mirrors everywhere, mirrors in which all things blur and vanish but the face of the beholder. Jack was her blood—her grandson, she believes—though still she would own to that only privately.

Nonetheless, she will not let him wander from care.

48. Episode: Kommós

(Manent MUSES, who move to stage left. They are joined by T. TOMMY BRISCOE, who stands downstage right)

Melpomene: They call it the *kommós*. A lament in the tragedy, a song shared by the actors and the chorus. It appears near the end of the play, at the play's catastrophe—when Oedipus blinds himself, when Orestes and Elektra stand over the murdered body of their mother, when Medea slaughters her children.

It is the song before the storm or after it, when the world catches its breath at the monstrousness of things.
(Thunder rumbles)

Tommy: Yes, children, sometimes you eat the god. And sometimes the god eats you. And some are called on account of rain.

Polymnia: Apache Downs and Billy Shepard, assigned crew duty by Stephen and George, begin to clear the stage as the Brischords settled on the lowest tier. Their Pentheus stands midstage, still brooding over his sister Maia, blonde hair stirring in an uncanny wind from the west, long cord hooked to his amplifier as the retro Stratocaster sputters.

He tunes to the sound of T. Tommy's voice.

Seven of them, teen and vagrant and in-between, wander the stage as a late spring rainstorm rushes toward the park from the west, bound east to spread across the Highlands and Crescent Hill, Queen Anne and Carpenter Gothic tangling in lightning and thunder and tepid June rain. The set is changing around them, as Apache and Billy remove Hamlet's mirrors, one of them dropped and broken over an altar of plankage and lumber.

Tommy: There was a time, back when I played a role in the economy—in the Clinton years, before Bush took back the country—when a prospect passed me by. Yes, an opportunity T. Tommy did not seize upon, if you can imagine. But this time I sinned through commission, not omission, and the world come down like this:

June or July of '94. I believe the white Bronco was still on the road, Al Cowlings at the wheel and the Juice in the back. I got the letter at my apartment, return address my darling Dhara, for whom I had distant yearnings ever since the '74 tornado uprooted me and whirled me about the city. Unfortunately it was a chain letter—no correspondence but the promise of riches and the threat that disaster would fall were I not to forward it to friends. And Daddy Chrome remembers, I am sure, don't shake your head, Chrome, you were one of my five correspondents, and you must of sent it along, else you would be derelict and where you are today.

Polymnia: The guitar springs into life, a melancholic blues riff girded with yearning and an unmoored passion. T. Tommy looks up and straight into the dolor of it, and he knows Vinnie DeChevre was swept to the heart of the blues, was passing close to something intimate and forbidden. Tommy dips the last of his pomade, welsh-combed it through his forelock, and continues.

Tommy: I did as it instructed, and I am here to thank the Lord and the King that not a penny came into my hands. Because I heard what transpired with Aurelius Wheat.

Named for the ancient emperor, the philosopher. Social worker himself, of girth and sparse beard, undistinguished in his walk across Broadway to his office, menthol Virginia Slim smoldering in one hand and Big Gulp coffee steaming in the other, brothers and sister. Lord knows he tried to heed his namesake, who said that the only *wealth* you will keep forever is what you have given away. So when he got the chain letter Aurelius did nothing, discarded the note and forgot about it until a lottery ticket rose on his horizons, a gift from a Vietnamese family he had guided through USCIS offices, more specifically from the sixteen-year-old son he would have guided luridly home were it not for a strong sense of Stoic ethics.

Aurelius had learned from his mother piety and beneficence, and abstinence, not only from evil deeds, but almost from evil thoughts. But the ticket come through. It brought him ten thousand dollars, and unhinged the simplicity of his living. But he remembered his ancestral wisdom, returning the money to the family he had helped, every dime of it, devoted to the education of that boy he would always watch chastely and from afar.

Of course, the family being family, money flowed from its original intent.

I understand that one of the cousins was pregnant by a much older white man, though there was a rumor that the daddy was more fierce and sinister and perhaps more glorious than just your average older white man. At any rate, she was abandoned now, and she needed the money for refuge and child care. Aurelius' young *amoroso* was more than glad to help his cousin, and Aurelius heard the story and understood, wishing there were more in his coffers to educate the boy, since the boy had given away all that Aurelius had given him.

Of course there ended up more, the story goes, because the impure and adrenalized excitement of the winning ticket had inveigled poor Aurelius, and oddly in search of its dregs he sent a two dollar trifecta bet on the ponies to Churchill via his supervisor, assured she would double his wager in a donation to Crusade for Children. He picked three names—Morning Star, Golden Touch, and Pan Pipe—because he found them 'cute', never reckoning odds or trainers or past performance, and astonished when they come in, finished in perfect order and brought him seven thousand fifty four dollars and change. He kept the fifty four and change, passed the seven on to the Nguyen family, and was not surprised when the boy directed it as seed money to his great-aunt's restaurant, the infant cousin by then having been taken into the supposed father's family, and the Vietnamese world north of the river settled into hard-working and thankful balance.

Until, of course, the rumbles xenophobic began, three restaurateurs raising public objections, wondering where Mai Nguyen had received financing, the trail of public record back to Aurelius' donations, the accusation of government financing and aberrant desire, the restaurant closing, Aurelius buckling under a job inquiry, his suspension with pay but also with confusion, media scrutiny, and humiliation. It led to a sad suicide, children, a cocktail of over-the-counter sleeping aids purchased with the $54.32 left over from the winning ticket, his savings funneled toward a burial on the family farm up near Central Barren, where parents embarrassed by the whole entanglement of Aurelius Wheat were consoled when the gravedigger, setting the site yards away from the family plot, uncovered soil that gave all signs of being oil-rich.

So Aurelius Wheat passed from the understanding of men, his opportunity tapped and tapped out. It is the god's doing: all of us ride the storm, its lessons slipping away even as they carry us back and forward, any place but here and now.

49. Episode: Just a Shot Away

(Thunder)

Polymnia: Tommy ends the story to Vincent's accompaniment as the wind rises over the park. The evergreens that line the western borders, the rise and tumble of the sculpted land as it abuts Sixth Street, all bend away from the diving gusts, and T. Tommy and the Brischords huddle in their funhouse of mirror and timber.

They sing against the tempest, a king in lamé and his tribe in exile. All the wind songs come to them— Dylan, Stevie Nicks, Jim Morrison's Riders—all the while the storm gaining traction, the high oak and poplar by the stage beginning to bow down in homage. *Come in, Tommy*, Falcon urges. *Come in, honey. Here's a night pities neither wise man nor fool.*

And Tommy, being both, shoulders off her hand and moves center stage in the downpour. He knows what lies backstage— cannot will not go there. But out here he smells the vintage of the tempest, and he glitters in rain-spackled augury, launching into the driving wail of the old levee song,

Tommy: *Cryin' won't help you, prayin' won't do you no good,*
Cryin' won't help you, prayin' won't do you no good,
When the levee breaks, mama, you got to move.

And it's comin'. Breath of the god in the air. They say 'bring him on' until he comes, and then the world falls out from under them and they wonder what the fuck they've done.

Polymnia: So he tells them, in time with the buck of Vinnie's Stratocaster. And then behind him, as if cued from the wings, the Keith Richards swampy hook from "Gimme Shelter" emergent, climbing the set like a vine, and the first lightning flare, shearing an oak limb over toward Fourth Street, and even Tommy is afraid, you could see it.

Tommy: Oh, naw, son, naw, get back into the lean-to.

Polymnia: and Vincent De Chevre recedes into the shadow, the music still driving, amplified and dangerously electric. In compromise to the storm, Daddy Chrome follows the boy and turns down the volume, as if somehow that will stop the current, but the riff continues.
Resigned, T. Tommy joins in at the second verse:

Tommy: *Ooh, see the fire is sweepin'*
My very street today
Burns like a red coal carpet
Mad bull lost its way

Polymnia: as the other four, Vinnie singing backup as well, slide into the chorus, because now they all know in a space under knowing that it was, indeed, just a shot away.

Clio: It is Maia, of course, who has brought Vinnie to this. Her confession on the stage that morning has unpinned his moorings, and he has wandered through the afternoon impelled on a dark wind he does not understand until sunset. But the gods are friends to such shadows: Kronos and Rhea, and their children Zeus and Hera. And parent and child, like Myrhha and Theas, like Oedipus and Mama. The offspring doomed like someone has garbled the genetic code.

Erato: Vinnie still backs away from the knowledge. Even tells himself that it has to do with Jack, that the new friendship with the dark and golden boy has a hint of the letch in it. He pushes the truth backstage, where it coils and watches him from behind transparent scales.

Clio: But by sunset he has owned what he is up against. Vincent comes to the stage as the storm brews and surges east up the river, begins to play only when he hears T. Tommy speak, inventing atop the scalding undertow of old Zepplin songs. And now, backing Tommy's broken wail, missing Jack's bottom to the great and ominous Stones song, he turns the corner toward resolution, riding the night and telling himself, no doubt, that everything will all be all right, that it would all pass.

Polymnia: Taking the song through all of its threats now, through war and rape and murder and flood, Vinnie plays on, his thoughts fastened to the rhythm of the riff and to that rhythm only, riding the snake as Tommy and the Brischords wail the final chorus and the wind screams over them all.

He must feel the unraveling. Like a ghost in a sarcophagus right before it fragments into the vital, undefining flow, Vinnie must be passing through a moment of knowing what is happening, must step from the shadows slowly to see himself reflected manifold in the fractured mirror. To see the vine rising to claim the stage and T. Tommy hustles for cover as the lightning crashes and shears a branch not twenty yards beyond them, and the windows on the court rattle with the heavy, pursuant thunder.

(The thunder subsides. We are all safe. The second part of the play is over. Exeunt omnes).

50. Episode: First Aftermath

(Enter POLYMNIA and THE MUSES.)

Clio: Seven days and not a sign. The police combing the park, the surrounding streets to no trace of Vincent De Chevre. The family as bereft as all families are in these circumstances. The media, on the other hand, baffled as to how to present the tragedy: Vincent is or was young and blonde and white, but he is male, so the traditional coverage of candlelit vigils, internet photos, maternal pleas, and high school students hugging one another to the strains of "Amazing Grace" no longer apply, as the city struggled with a new language for abduction.

Of course, the search continues. The police go to work, leads trailing into urban myths of vanishing hitchhikers and alien impressments. A group of indigents questioned fruitlessly, announcements from Peter Koenig's pulpit and George's and Dolores' lecterns, students talking to students, Madeleine Rausch talking to her people, who talk to theirs. Everyone talking to the police except the people at Fourth and Fellini. And the people at that corner of chaos full of opinion and knowhow, every cyclist's and loiterer's advice cut with rock and witchery.

Ganymede. Europa. Persephone. Orion. For generations the gods have snatched mortals, and though we should know better ourselves, we gossip and speculate like the fourth estate in a funhouse.

Thalia: I am sure he will turn up. Haven't the rest of them, all along? Isn't the story about rescue, about going to fetch the hostage, as the De Chevres themselves had done when they released Jack Rausch from Antioch and the prisons of Grover's Corners?

Melpomene: My dear little ingénue sister…in all such stories, even in the Rausch rescue, none of the hostages return home. They are placed among the gods or endure the fiery, scattering change into constellations. Glamorous, indeed, but no longer among their mortal families mourning and bereft.

Erato (*brushing back her anarchy of hair, her green eyes shining feverishly*): It's all about love and desire. Somehow the god wants Vincent De Chevre, like he wanted Ampelos back in that distant, exploratory time of divine adolescence. To what purpose we cannot be sure, but Vincent is beautiful and gifted, after all, and blessed with golden ringlets that rival those of his sister for color and allure. Those are the kind of youths desired by unmanageable forces, boys who end poorly because they are beloved.

Clio: So much for motive. Bring me evidence. Bring me forensics. The police collar T. Tommy and the Brischords the morning after the storm, dump them back at Fourth and Fellini after only a few hours interrogation. Tommy is holding court from there, is back among his people and joining the chorus of testimony, his opinion carrying more weight because he was there. And though T. Tommy did not see the vanishing, he had picked up in its aftermath, seen the boy reflected in two dozen shards of mirror, simulacra held in the startled glass so that even next morning a police detective, cynical and smart and subject to no delusion, sent some of the fragments back to the lab for evidence, for anything.

Polymnia: Some of my sisters choose not to debate, but crouch in the storm-ruined branches, sprouting feathers as they listen to the others go on, their black wings gleaming in the sunlight. There was a time when the gods punished girls by transforming them into magpies: for telling false stories that impugned them. But now, working changes on themselves for celerity and concealment, the girls rise aflutter from the wreckage of trees and soar north over tennis courts and Park Avenue, over Ormsby's rows of houses until they see the intersection, the orbiting bicycles and the slow, linear push of traffic. Here they sit themselves down to listen, watch, and bode.

And there the debates continue, and words take the place of discovery.

51. Episode: Shock Brings Progress

Polymnia: On the ninth day after Vinnie's translation, Stephen meets with survivors at his apartment. A shaken Aron, accompanied by his mother. George Castille, who cautions everyone against haste: *I know the show must go on, dears, but let's wait until the body count is reckoned, shall we?* Maia De Chevre is understandably absent, adrift in the wreckage of her family. To George's dismay, Stephen is replacing her as well.

Stephen feels forced to decisions. His augury was *Chên*, the sign of shock and thunder and arousing:

> *Shock brings progress*
> *Shock comes in laughter*
> *It terrifies for a hundred miles*
> *The sacrificial vessel is not lost*

All of this sounds good, a consolation over losses. But it is an unstable hexagram: the lines move like faults in earthquake country. Six in the second place again cautions loss of all treasures, climbing the nine hills, whatever that means. But he will recover those losses, it tells him, in seven days.

Such recovery is heartening, and yet the dropped lines continue to complicate readings, the possibilities bifurcating again. An unstable line in the fifth place predicts the shock spreading. He thinks of the '08 earthquake, his apartment jostled until the books dropped from the cinderblock shelves. Again he is told no harm, no foul.

The sixth place was the most complicated. *Shock brings ruin*, it told him,

> *and breathless dismay*
> *If it has first reached your neighbors*
> *there is no blame*

Dolores suggests that Maia be given time. That after all…

Stephen bristles at her look, reminds her that tragedy or no, the dress rehearsal is only two weeks away, the opening night a week after. Too many people have staked their dreams and even their livelihoods.

But Vincent played *Pentheus*, George advises him. A major role, perhaps *the* major role. As many lines as the god. How, in the short space of a fortnight, could he expect teenaged memory to take them in, much less turn water into Dionysian wine?

It is a sticking point. Lacking passable young actors, Stephen has played out a tricky system of backup and understudy. Now the part of Agave is frankly up for grabs: Maia's understudy is a high-school girl who cannot shake a nasal, South End twang. The other options are little better: in the event of Aron's illness or absence, Jack Rausch is to assume the role. Would that Aron were the one missing, Stephen thinks before catching himself with a shudder. It is a horrible thought, and furthermore, Apache Downs is his backup Pentheus, and the thought of such change in the starring roles is karma enough for ill thinking.

For a moment he almost gives in to George and Dolores. After all, there are other years. Defeated by the chaos, he has fallen back already on *The Music Man* for next year's performance. Its cheer and full-volume American innocence are what the crowd really wanted and what *he* yearns for by now, swept in the growing awareness that Euripides is too much for him, all that apocalypse and omophagy that could slip through his hands. He could replace the violent god with trombones and patriotic parades, and nobody would know the difference.

So he almost gives in, so close to spilling the sacrificial vessel.

Thalia: Then Dolores—almost reluctantly, or so it seems—offers herself for the part of Agave.

Stephen should have seen it coming. From her high school teaching to marshalling her son's scattered talents, all the way to taking in Jack Rausch, she has grown, since he first knew her, into the role of rescuer. And now she will play a sacrificial vessel, giving up that dream of ingénue roles, of romantic leads, to play the mother she is. Never mind she had just defended Maia De Chevre to upstage her only minutes later: Dolores was a professional, a professional is always on call, and he is forced to buy into this performance.

So he praises her at once, and was gratified when George, richly attuned to all kinds of theatrical ego, points out the nuance and depth that Dolores can bring to the role that Maia, despite some talent, is too inexperienced to gather.

Melpomene: One problem dodged, then. But Apache Downs, all sulk and blemishes, is a Pentheus that makes Stephen shudder, that he had never considered possible because Vincent was so reliable and apparently healthy. There is something he hopes, something that danced at the edge of saying when he and George originally discussed the cast. Now, their prospects narrowed to three weeks' time and several perilous options, Stephen hopes Aron will do the right thing.

But to Stephen's great relief, Dolores, in her newfound role as rescuer, suggests the shift. She points out that Aron, who has stood the stage in reading and rehearsal with Vinnie De Chevre and learned the part of the prince with that of the god, might step into the other principal role. Jack Rausch has been present and prepared at every practice, his talent shown to be workmanlike at Antioch. He could do a passable god at once, and might, with some coaching (which she would provide) rise to a strong performance.

And just think, she offers. In Aron's debut as the principal tragic role, the principal actor in the play, mother and son will be *actual* mother and son. It had a note of the inevitable about it, she assures Aron Starr, whose eyes slowly widen with rage and betrayal.

52. Episode: Muriel's Dream

Thalia: She is on about *The Glass Menagerie* when he picks up the phone again.

Stephen had last left his mother preaching the virtues of *The Cherry Orchard.* Over the last few days, in a number of phone calls, Muriel Thorne has second-guessed his choice of *The Bacchae*, running through *Uncle Vanya* and *Hedda Gabler,* reprising her own list of credits as though, at eighty-seven, she is being considered for the role. At one time, he hung up on her when she opened the conversation with how they *could compromise:*

You can do your Euripides, as long as it's Medea.

He has never considered Caller ID, thinking there was something furtive and cowardly about screening calls. But this time the calls are different. Muriel and Stephen are meeting on a ground they hold in common, and she sees it as power struggle. When he calls her on despotism, she shrinks back, becomes the long-suffering mother, sweet, elderly, and oh so fragile, whose

227

son has cast her onto the altar of his ego.

Frustrated at every turn, he has gone to advisors. Certain that George Castille, about five years his elder, must have undergone the same torment with the formidable Amanda, he has asked his old friend how he had endured the trial.

Oh, honey, you simply outlive her, George replied, his eyes rolling back with the memory. *You just wait until she dies.*

Nor does the next advisor console. *I Ching* presents smugly the hexagram of the Marrying Maiden, which bodes of *undertakings bringing misfortune* and *nothing that would further*. Whether these doomed endeavors are hers or his, the yarrow sticks does not say, but honed instinct and maternal history tells him not to take it up, not to meet her on stage.

He smiles when he speaks into the phone again. Knows she can hear it, that it will disarm her. She is in mid-speculation as to whether he could have a worse choice of play. Has decided he could, but finds herself hard-pressed to name it.

The Libation Bearers, Stephen offers. To her questioning pause, he adds that it was the one where Orestes comes back for vengeance and kills his mother.

A still longer pause forewarns him, so he absorbs rather calmly her claim that indeed she knew *The Libation Bearers* and was just waiting to see if he could have meant it so cruelly.

So my bastard grandson is still playing Bacchus? she asks slyly, and again Stephen feels compelled to correct her, to assure that Aron is no blood of hers, that there is no reason to doubt that Robert Starr was the father. Is told he should have married that poor girl, made her honest and given that son a name and better genes. Told again how wrong he has done her.

So he points out Dolores's track record: himself and Starr and, from what he had heard, several in between, including the Reverend Peter Koenig, a name he conjures because Muriel loathes the man.

Like many actresses, he points out, Dolores Webb had trouble keeping a man.

Polymnia: *You should never have kidnapped that boy, Stephen. Koenig is a vengeful soul and you are no match for his power,* Muriel warns her son. *But I did not call to lecture.*

I wanted to tell you about the dream I had.

As usual, Stephen cannot tell whether her accounts of dreams are genuine or whether she invents them as she goes along. It almost always seems that her dreams teach her son a lesson, that the vast network of the subconscious conspires with Muriel Thorne against him. So when her dream involves a visit to the Park Theatre on a brilliant summer night, Stephen suspects that it will conclude with Hedda Gabler's walk out on stage, beckoning for Muriel to emerge from the wings, and exchanging clothes with her while her son exchanges scripts with Ibsen, doing what is only right in the final hours before dress rehearsals.

But instead, in her dream Muriel walked through the backstage silence. Brushed a gloved hand against scenery flats and examined the red, powdery crust against her fingertips. And there was a stairway, she claims, leading down below the stage, and following it, her hands spread before her in the dark, she heard the soft crackle of cobwebs breaking and felt the pull of vine and root against her arms and ankles. The air as she descended became warmer, stank of shallow river and the harsh, metallic smell of fluvial life.

And she heard the rustle of moist leaves, the slog of something stirring in mud, and from some indefinite source—moon or lamp or candle—a faint light spilled and glistened over slowly undulant scales, over something coiled at the foot of the stairs.

It is a warning, she tells him. Her dream foretells danger.

He assures her, thereby assuring himself, that the theatre has no cellar, that it sits on solid earth and that its roots drive deep into old and stable soil. But as he tells her good night, as he invites her to attend the dress rehearsals he hopes she will pass up, he catches himself looking out the apartment window, across the court and into the deep, foreboding enticement of the trees.

53. Episode: Again Maia, Again No

Polymnia: The time races toward the dress rehearsals. Swamped by duties, by the handling of the cast, Stephen relies more and more on coffee to raise him in the morning, vodka to lull him at night. A half-hearted attempt to lure Maia De Chevre back to the production fails miserably: she refuses to see him, and her family backs her fiercely. The hunt continues for Vinnie De Chevre, but it has been two weeks since he vanished, and everyone suspects that a window of time has opened and closed.

T. Tommy and the Brischords return to their haunts in the park, having ducked the LMPD and persuaded the detectives that their only guilt lies in being the last to see Vinnie De Chevre. As vagrants in good standing, they know someone who knows someone related to someone, and by that chain of knowledge and their also-known intake of alcohol and God knows what else, they persuade the police that their testimony is already no more than urban legend.

Jack Rausch is brought in once, then questioned again when

the leads dry up. Both times he goes willingly, his demeanor serene. He extends his hands for cuffs, and the cops confess they are only bringing him as procedure, because he had been absent from the regular music session on that night and that night alone. Surprisingly, and even with a kind of sober cheer, Jack stands up under sorrow and civic pressure, staying with rehearsals until George and Dolores bring the matter up to Stephen, saying that even if Jack doesn't look suspicious, the repeated questioning does. But to Stephen the boy is beyond misgiving: he learns his lines, works well with T. Tommy and the Brischords, who remains the intended chorus despite George, who says *to hell with innovation and with your all-consuming desire to offend, these days you get women to play the maenads, god damn it, and I can have you five community college girls who can remember lines and chant in unison on short notice.*

Until Stephen concedes, said he will back off, pay the derelicts $100 and three bottles of Richards *if and only if we can find a chorus leader worth her salt.*

Melpomene: Which is why he goes again to the De Chevre place, this time with Jack Rausch in tow.

Maia receives them from the top of the stairs, Jack having charmed his way past the parents whose grief has turned to cool hostility. But Maia smiles at him, and shakes her head, either incredulous at his nerve or already saying no to whatever he asked.

But the smile raises Stephen's hopes. Like a good director, he backs toward the door, marveling at how sweetly Jack approaches the girl. Marveling as well that, of the two, Jack Rausch just might be the more beautiful.

But no, Maia says. And again, no.

Jack is done with questioning. On the way home he watches the road before them, his eyes veiled by sunglasses, his face inscrutable. Amiably he dodges questions, which become more probing, more personal, and even more futile as Stephen parks the car at the curb and the two of them walk down the winding sidewalk toward the amphitheater, to be met by George Castille, who lays out further trouble.

54. Episode: A Note of Dischord

Polymnia: What George brings to him is news—news of the first open rupture between mother and son.

For almost two weeks, Aron has sulked and resisted. He learns the lines, but cannot break through to the character. He threatens the god and the maenads, does it with all the force Euripides put in the words two millennia past, but he is still not Pentheus, not quite there in heart and imagination. Between scenes he stands in the wings, smoking and lowering.

Stephen looks to George. The play has come unmoored with the vanishing of Vincent De Chevre. No Pentheus, no music. Aron has dragged it into a series of words and motions, and now it drifts off course in the last, perilous week before the dress rehearsals.

Now Stephen keeps the cast late. Now he hashes through the problems with a baffled George and Dolores. It is clear that Pentheus and Agave are at great discord, clear by the way Aron delivers the first, scornful speech of the Theban prince:

I left my kingdom briefly, but the tidings
of mischief in the city reached me there.
I heard the Theban women left their homes
feigning the rites of Bacchus, honoring
some Dionysos in the wooded hills.
The krater stands among them, one by one
they steal away with boys to lonely spots
and gratify their itches, still pretending
it is all Bacchic ritual, when in fact
it's Aphrodite to their cloven crotches.

Dolores feels menaced by it. She feels looked in upon, like Aron is spying or judging. More than anything—even more than her son's well-being, she wants to be the "cool mom" that Aron's friends, especially Jack, claim she is. Aron has re-directed the words from Pentheus' bruised Puritanism to a kind of peeping-tom obsession with the imagined hot itches of his own mother.

It is no place in which Dolores Starr can picture herself.

When she returns home the night before dress rehearsals, the message from her son surprises only the best impressions she has of herself. It is taped inside the refrigerator door, to the compartment in which she keeps the meat. She sets the raw steak on the counter and spreads the note. Two pages as harsh and venomous as any words of Pentheus'.

Aron speaks of his father, like on rare occasions. But he moves beyond that, with unnatural intuitions, and calls her out on Koenig and on Stephen before him. His sharp eye uncovers and does not forgive, does not take into account that Dolores' history is history. And still the note continues, its intuitions wilder and deeper:

Don't lie any more, Dolores, you have a
checkered past and no decency. It's all
hella clear that you haven't stopped yet,
you took my part away, bitch, you made
me mortal so you could get your cougar

claws on Jack, didn't you, and my only
consolation in this is that he dont want
your old ass, he may of stolen my gf
but he is a dog not a retard and I can
live with him as long as he don't hook
up with you, which he won't. So go
ahead and play my mother, you cunt,
it's a hard role for you but go thru the
motions tear me in pieces like Agave
does in the play and just be sure I
will see to it you won't hook up with
someone young enough to be your son.

It is hard to read, hard to imagine it thought.

She sets aside the knife and fork she had brought to the counter, begins to tear the uncooked meat with her fingers, her thoughts on the accusation as she brings her dripping fingers to her mouth.

And something further, coiled deep in her thoughts, surfaces in what she thinks at first is sadness that Jack Rausch has stolen her son's girlfriend. But instantly, and with horror, Dolores recognizes she is not sad for her son or for the girl, but for herself.

Melpomene: She leaves Aron a note and walks where she needs to go, a winter shawl wrapped around her shoulders though the June night is warm. The hardware shop on Oak Street has a shattered window boarded up, a solitary light on as the owner, his tools available in the aisles, repairs the damage from the third break-in of the year. A woman squats on a porch across from the nursing home and glares as Dolores passes, her toddler son ranging up and down the stairs, awake and out past reasonable bedtime.

Sure that somewhere some kind of god is watching, Dolores clutches her son's note, folded in the pocket of her jeans, and follows the lights toward the next intersection where a small crowd mills beneath a Rite Aid sign, their conversation raucous like a boding of ravens. Three of the women she thinks she recognizes, all better dressed than those she generally sees in passing when she drives from Third to Fifth at a quick cruise, the doors locked and the windows up.

Then the fourth she knows. Blonde scattering of hair, the image of her brother in shorts and hoodie, weaving on her feet. Maia as *marijuanera* courted by a brace of brothers and bantering in her father's worst nightmare. Of course she recognizes Ms. Starr at once, but calls her Dolores and motions her in.

And over the pavement Dolores comes to her, as the gods watch with curiosity spiked and disinterested.

(Exeunt).

55. Stasimon: Strophe: Brothers on Bicycles

(Enter T. TOMMY BRISCOE.)

T. Tommy: Brothers on bicycles. Sign of the wound and the revel. Pedaling aimlessly through the city, economically shaken out and dropped on purpose. I know the numbers: life expectancy and child mortality, diseases communicable and chronic, hypertension and small-arms fire.

Two blocks from here are drawing rooms that match old times for opulence. There are three floors of housing for a childless couple, riding mowers for city lots. There is stained glass in windows—original to the buildings, they tell the photographers—and that glass minded more carefully than you mind me, my Brischords, or than this city minds its generation of cyclists.

There was a time in everybody's childhood when a body

might sacrifice dove or goat or holocaust of beeves. For which the gods would lay down treasures. We still see such deals cut among Mafia dons and Evangelical Prosperity Gospel, where you jimmy the old causal machinery, so that every time it rains, it rains pennies from heaven.

They claim that there's a pattern of things you might of seen from a helicopter high above this intersection, where these brothers on bicycles hint at a larger design, something you might catch hold of from a single engine plane, or maybe as far as a weather satellite might get you. But that, too, is a momentary stay against confusion, a truce with the world. Because the world, children, is alive with nonexistent gods, a place where last week's storm took away our young guitarist in mid-shred. A world that reconfigured after that sadness like the streets return to normal when a cyclist falls in a hidden alley. Somewhere a tenant got evicted or a WalMart clerk laid off, or on one of them occasions of balance and design, a more useless denizen was lifted into spectacular and unforeseen light.

Out of what seems to be disorder, order and structure fake an emergence. That is, if you squint your eyes right and you catch them in perfect light. There are no identical snowflakes, but they all have six sides, like the hexagonal papers of the Starr boy's game map, like our own ground, darlings, where the vine bleeds and grows.

56. Stasimon: Antistrophe: Polymnia, Muses, Maia, Beverly Nguyen

(Enter POLYMNIA and the MUSES. Enter into the orchestra MAIA and BEVERLY NGUYEN)

Polymnia: Our numbers swell now, sisters. Two mortals join us, standing before us, one step below our song, in troubled sleep among the audience. So let this stage be a bloodstained mountain in Boeotia, where many creatures have fallen to the hunter. Let it be the mountain at high mid-day 'You think,' he said, 'it is the spirit of the elements, and I thought perhaps it was the old gods. But I tell you now it is – neither. These would be comprehensible entities, for they have relations with men, depending upon them for worship or sacrifice, whereas these beings who are now about us have absolutely nothing to do with mankind, and it is mere chance that their space happens just at this spot to touch our own.'

Melpomene: There the hunter Actaeon tells his friends to call it a day, their spears and nets dripping. When the dawn comes, they will resume, he tells them, but for now the air is hot and still. Finish your task, he says. Call in the dogs, piss on the fire, and seek the shade.

Polymnia: Nearby is a valley sacred to the goddess. There, in the depths, lies a wooded cave, where nature has made an arch out of pumice and limestone, mixing fire and water in a kind of narcotic artifice. Here the goddess Artemis bathes in a shadowy pool. While attendants loosen her hair, she looks into the water, where the moonlight slants against the surface. She sees her serene, Platonic face shaped by an image beneath it, an abstract violence giving it form and structure, the terrible innocence of a child warrior. As her servants help her out of her tunic, she imagines faces behind the face in the water, the face in the framing moon. Perplexities of light resolve to face upon face, an infinite regression, a sign of the immortal in her.

Melpomene: While she bathes there, Actaeon strays through the wood, never noticing the stillness. As soon as he reaches the cave mouth, it yawns to permit his entry, the entry of light. Now the attendants of the goddess, seeing a man's face, beat at their breasts and fill the whole wood with their sudden outcry. They crowd round Artemis to hide her with their bodies. But the goddess stands head and shoulders above all the others, her face the color of sun-stained clouds. She catches a handful of the water, and throws it over Actaeon's head...

Polymnia: And he begins to change. The stag horns sprout painfully, the hands transforming, cleaving, Actaeon's skin dappling as he falls to all fours and begins to run. The forest alters: the once-distant birds now open and clamorous, the light a transparency of leaf and shadow. Now the masted and rooted ground rolls beneath his swift feet and for a moment he feels exuberance, almost joy. Until his dogs catch sight of him, and he knows.

Melpomene: Now he runs across the country where he has often hunted, this time flying from his own hounds. He longs to shout 'I am Actaeon! Know your own master!' but he only groans, and the air echoes to the baying. Now they surround him on every side, sinking their jaws into his flesh, tearing their master to pieces in the deceptive shape of the deer. The whole pack gathers, and they shred and rend till there is no place left to wound him. Actaeon cries out, a painful, half-bestial cry, and wishes he could shake this burden from himself—this knowing, this invention of death more painful and frightful than the jaws of his hounds, against which all devices of faith and art are torn asunder.

But who is this now before us? Who stands before us in disarray, hair tangled with darkness and hands interwoven? Who looks out and up to us, reflections pooled in a shambles of mirror?

(BEVERLY NGUYEN and MAIA DeCHEVRE step onto the stage, helped up by POLYMNIA and MELPOMENE.)

Beverly: We hold hands across generations, across fractured light and being and unbeing. This pretty girl, Jack, who dreamed you into light. Who shared with you the *qeej* around your neck and its story—my story to you, Jack, of broken reeds made whole and lyric in the prince's hands. But now my body breaks reeds along the riverbank, slowly moving like the goddess bathing or like Hamlet's crazy girl. A fisherman my Actaeon, discovering me downstream, washed against the pylon of the Matthew Walsh

Bridge, my body liquescent and transformed. And all talk of foul play sweeps down the current, passing toward shadow and the Mississippi, scattered in the wake of the approaching night, the approaching god.

Now I am indifferent, afloat on a current that has erased my breath, then memory and awareness, then identity as I dissolve into the undertow.

Maia: I would have been something splendid in your eyes, because you awakened me, Jack. It was like I was lying on a slab of stone somewhere, all shadowy in full sunlight. Or like a painted figure, recumbent on an ancient clay vessel. Then your voice lifted me out of sleep, and I know now where I am headed. And no, do not smile at me that lovely smile, because you will get no traction from it, not now. I am headed out to the crossroads to twist snakes in my hair—isn't that from the chorus you want me to lead, Mr. Thorne? Yes, I am headed out, because I saw the summons that night from my brother's van, when we brought Elvis to the corner and the light seemed to spread across all that sadness and desertion. There is a place for us—for me—out there, and I will not be alone.

So go along, sweet Jack. We'll meet soon. This will end in bliss and you know it.

(Exeunt MAIA, BEVERLY NGUYEN, THE MUSES. Manet POLYMNIA).

57. Episode: Jack

Polymnia: Sunset at the theater. Jack stands naked at the foot of the Witches' Tree, over there at the far corner of the park, looking across the promenade and over the tiered benches to where the stage stands, bathed by the moon, the theater lights dormant this evening.

The stone lions stir lazily, guarding the short colonnade that leads from nowhere to nowhere, as Jack reaches up, grabs a low branch of the maple, and begins to climb through the moonlight, his hair longer than we remember, oiled and tumbling onto his shoulders.

He will not remember what transpires. Only that we encircle him now, at concentric distances, Muse after Muse regarding him from a hundred feet away, from a block, from four blocks, from a mile, our clothing disheveled, vines in our hair, shouting *euoi*, a cry of adoration, not so much for Jack Rausch as the element he now embodies. The cry rises from the north, from Fourth and Fellini, from the west where the last hint of sun settles on the low roofs of the projects, from the south where Tommy is awakening after a short sleep at the bus stop and where, not a hundred yards from where he lies, the calyx on the second floor of the art museum is bare now, because the god is free from the surface of the vase, is wandering the concentric streets north toward the theater, the omphalos, the center of the city's rotating world.

And alone in the night, Jack waits, surrounded by our song, breathing in the god, who lifts him up through the branches, where he can see it all. The women assembled at the street corner to the north, Aron pacing his apartment to the west, and to the south the wind rushing toward him, the leaves turning silver backs toward a rain that will not come tonight. Infused by the god, *enthousiastikos,* he sees them all finding their mark on the larger stage of the city, in a scene that begins wide and expansive, then narrows in swift time to the amphitheater, to the stage, to the performance that approaches with swift inevitability.

Jack knows it will not end well. What is left of Jack, that is. Soon he forgets that doomed amusement, because the deep and powerful entity that moves his graceful body through the branches does not hold with happy endings. Instead, the god looks out through Jack's eyes, regarding a handful of people who wander the streets or sleep restlessly already, who will make their way to the stage and the sacrifice soon, too soon.

Jack's smile is inscrutable. His thoughts descend on nothing. His hair trembles in a hot wind.

58. Episode: Peripateia

Polymnia: The next morning Stephen receives a panic-stricken call from Aron.

Dolores has not come home. When Aron had come in a little after midnight to find the apartment empty, he assumed she was out late planning for the play, would be in when he awoke the next morning. Out of suspicion he had tossed the mail onto her bed, and was alarmed to find it there, in the same spot, when he awoke at noon.

Stephen is at a loss. Her phone goes straight to voicemail, and the people who might know her whereabouts—the college where she taught a summer class, the occupant of the next door apartment, her best friend at the high school—all have no word of her since yesterday morning.

George Castille is no help, either. "Oh, you know Dolores. She's on a drunk somewhere and I can already feel the flop sweat." He wails into the phone, hysterical despite Stephen's attempts to soothe him.

"Surely she is all right," Stephen says, more to himself than to George. But it feels as though all disaster is converging on the park, on the theatre, jostling his unsteady designs, and Stephen is already to the end of his resources.

The police could be of no help, he tells himself, still believing that the twenty-four-hour waiting period applied to all missing persons. As a long shot—one that fails—he tries contacting Maia De Chevre to fill in for the dress performance, but as the hours move up through the afternoon he tries Dolores again.

This time she answers sleepily. Slides away from Stephen's outrage. Will not tell him where she has been, but assured him she is well, will be present and accounted for that night. An odd way of saying it, but everything about her sounds odd, disengaged, and he writes it off as another long carousal, makes her promise to set an alarm for five so she can be at the theatre by sunset.

59. Episode: The Anointing

(Enter Melpomene. Manet POLYMNIA. The two stand center stage, facing each other. We are no longer in their regard. The sisters speak quietly, the lights low).

Melpomene: Aron arrives an hour early to rehearse lines with Jack. There is the scene between Dionysos and Pentheus, charged with intense dialogue, where the adolescent prince, self-righteous and egocentric, tries and fails to face down the god. Aron does not want to rehearse it. There is something too explosive and intimate about it.

He finds Jack up there, in the topmost tier of the amphitheater.

Jack cocks his head and smiles, as though he has summoned Aron out of the air. "I figure by now," he says, "we should be ready. If we don't know the lines, the play's pretty much fucked anyway, now isn't it?"

Surprised at Jack's language and indifference, Aron sits beside him nonetheless. He wants to object, to maintain that far from it, the play will be all right, just fine. But he catches himself before he disagrees. After all, Mr. Castille has told him to use the discomfort he felt around Jack. To remember that Pentheus and Dionysos, though family, are no friends. He wishes Jack would just go away until "places", because hanging around him makes Aron forget hostilities.

Polymnia: "Then I'll go on, Jack," he says, perhaps a little abruptly. "Gotta roust Mom anyway. She sleeps through alarms."

"Oh, she's awake," Jack replied.

"How would you…"

"Saw her on the way over here. Passed by Fourth and Fellini, and she was there by the Rite Aid."

"Jack, that ain't funny. That's my mom." Aron paused. "Why were you there anyway? Looking for Maia?"

"It's the last place anyone saw Vincent," Jack replied. Then, smiling enigmatically, "…or maybe not. Right?"

They are both silent for a moment, then Aron whispers, "God, Jack. What's happening? Is everybody gonna fuckin' vanish?"

"Oh, your mom was very visible, Aron."

"What does that mean?"

"Means out in front of the Rite Aid. Hanging with some of the women there." Jack laughed. "I actually saw one of my aunts. Ina, I think. They all look alike with sunglasses."

"How about Maia?" Aron asks. "Did you see her?"

"She wants nothing to do with me, Aron. To be honest, I wasn't even looking. But it isn't pretty down there right now. Your mom and my aunts are there. Maybe Maia. I think they've had their fill of the men, and I can't say as I blame them. They've picked up a couple of bottles of Sutter Home, are sitting on that brick wall next to the Family Dollar and the beauty supplies place. Trying on wigs and taunting the brothers. The police came by and dispersed them, but they gathered again. It's like they all circle wildly but if you stand at a height—like in a tree at the edge of the park, or ,for you, in the bell tower of the Methodist

Church just north of them—and you watched them circle, you'll see a pattern forming in it, a large design…"

"We gotta get her out of there, Jack," Aron insists.

Melpomene: But Jack shakes his head. "Getting strange down there. Dunno how welcome a boy would be among 'em, Aron. Any boy. Even a son."

Aron stands, makes as though to leave. "Don't be dumb, Jack. It's my mom."

"And what did you say in the note, Aron? What'd you call her? What'd you accuse her of?"

Aron sits back down. How Jack would know these things does not cross his mind. "We need her here. It's only an hour till they start to gather for dress rehearsal. People will be here, Jack."

"Is that all it is, Aron? No other reason?"

The two of them regard each other across a wide, inscrutable gulf.

"You need to go get her," Jack says at last. "Not me. She's *your* mom, after all. But come along. I'll help you."

60. Episode: Processional

Polymnia: So Jack prepares him for the journey, there backstage in the hour before rehearsals.

Aron objects to the change of clothing. There will be time when he had returned with Dolores. There is no need to wear the tunic yet, certainly no need for the makeup. It makes him feminine, takes away his power.

While he dresses Prince Pentheus in the layers of costume and drag, Jack tells the boy about Herakles, who served Queen Omphale in purple robe and slippers as penance for family murders. About Achilles, who was hidden from recruiters by his mother, dressed in the clothes of princesses to duck the drafting eye of Odysseus.

But this is not the old days, Aron argues, wrestling as Jack slipped the tunic over his shoulders. *We're just playing this, and it's Louisville in the 21st century, after all.*

Heracles and Achilles, Aron, is Jack's only argument. *Passing through couture and coming out heroes, what's cooler than that?*

Hold still before I blind you with eyeliner.

They'll tear me apart over there, Aron objects, gesturing vaguely north toward the intersection where he is told he will find his mother, Jack's aunts, even Maia.

(Enter THE MUSES, joining their sisters center stage)

And now our sisters emerge from the castoff sets, rising from the fragments of mirrors swept into a disheveled heap backstage, the mirrors into which Vincent had fallen out of body.

Erato and Thalia *(in unison)*: Aron Starr, how fabulously you meet the occasion. Frocked and bouffanted in the twilit park, you could almost be lovely were you not destined for valor.

Melpomene: We shall see. We shall see where valor takes him. *(Aside to the audience)* I already know. My uncertainty is just narration.

Polymnia: The boys walk a ways north together, and it never occurs to Aron to ask for further company, for backup. Something about his bravery might appeal to Maia, he tells himself. The air stirs with promise, and he catches the smell, commingled with smoke and diesel, as he reaches Fourth and Ormsby and looks into the light. Half a block ahead, there by the bus stop, dark silhouettes mesh with shadow. The world is slipping out of definition, but Jack lays his hand on Aron's shoulder and suddenly fear is a narcotic, an enticement, not the truth of what lies behind this lonely impulse of curiosity and delight. *I will show them all and be someone*, Aron thinks defiantly.

Thalia: *(laughs)*. Aron, Aron. *That* never ends well.

Erato: How do you mean, dearest?

Thalia: "Showing them all and being someone."

Melpomene: Hush, both of you. Aron is hearing things.

He hears Jack's words commingling with his thoughts: he is already *someone*, just not who he thought he would be.

Jack leaves him the north side of the street, at the doorstep of the old Puritan building and across from the former bank. Now Aron moves alone toward the corner, where the transactions are loud, the lights brilliant. To his left it seems like two suns setting over a line of brownstones, and as he looks back into the confusion of slanted sunlight and the rising glow of the streetlamps a glimmer catches Jack's hair, which seems to coil and harden and rise as though he is horned or helmeted. Nonetheless Aron wishes Jack would stay with him, would accompany him forward into the blinding and clamorous intersection.

Polymnia: Jack almost has to shout that he is leaving, is returning to the stage. When it registers with Aron above the din, a strange regret passes over and through him. He rushes back down the street toward Jack, shouts to him over the racket that all is forgiven, that he should be at peace and not worry.

Jack cocks his head, his smile distracting. He says he understands, that there is nothing to forgive, a perplexing reply to a perplexing statement, all of it lost in the loud, exhaustive sigh of a city bus, and when Aron cranes forward, asked him to repeat, Jack is gone, backing down the street with a warm, tidal wind lifting his jacket. He waves, turns, and strides into the baffled darkness.

Melpomene: And the noise surges around Aron, as harsh and driving as the wail of Vincent's reft guitar. He loses his mother in the milling people, looking vainly toward the store fronts for signs of Dolores, of Maia, but the faces blend with one another as though he sees the world through smoke or water, and the women by the drug store turn, and one points at him and shouts something.

Higher ground, Aron tells himself. *Jack said there was a vantage, and Tommy had said it before him: a point where you can watch the crowd mill and braid and tangle, where it almost makes sense.* He backs across Fourth through a rush of traffic, horns and the shriek of brakes and the cursing of drivers, finding himself somehow on the southeast corner of the intersection, next to the stone gothic arches of the Louisville Church of Christ. He presses his back against stone, finds purchase on a metal drain spout and begins to climb, gripping the spokes of the huge rose window that is a relic of some older time nobody remembers, a time of higher churches and architecture more devotional than industrial. And there aloft the building, Aron Starr looks down on the crowd approaching, scanning it for faces that will guide him home.

(All THE MUSES—POLYMNIA included—descend to the orchestra, where they stand facing the stage)

61. Episode: Sparagmos

(Enter T. TOMMY BRISCOE, dressed in full Elvis lamé and alone. THE MUSES look up, shield their eyes as though searching for something among the stage rafters).

Tommy: I will remember it, in the aftermath of that night and in the five years that yet remain to me. The sacrifice at Fourth and Fellini rises to join other memories, jostled to life by the boy on the church cornice, by the crowd milling below him.

I was standing in front of the Chinese take-out and looked on as the passing figures glided from actor to role, their shadows dilating and faltering against the streetlights as the old story rose out of their milling. It was like my dormant years—the time on the creek and in the cellars, riding the snake, Morrison and acid spiraling down to Richards' and park benches. It all come due at this intersection, where identity moved so fluidly that things were what they are but also what they might be.

Dolores or Queen Agave, still smarting from that letter penned by Pentheus or Aron, was down amongst the women, over by the Rite Aid sign dispensing Sutter Home in paper cups lifted from the store. She and the other women were opening their fourth bottle when the boy arrived. They were circled like one of them Protestant communions, everyone hunkered over separate little cups so that their mouths didn't touch where those of the others had.

The boy Pentheus stood by the bus stop, made his way up past the bank to the intersection and called out for mama, but Dolores was too drunk to recognize and almost too drunk to heed, weaving on her feet and joining the chorus of the corner girls to observe how *smooth* the wine was, each bottle *smoother* than the one before.

So Aron called out again, and from my vantage near the tattoo shop just north of the Chinese restaurant, I could barely hear the calling over the crowd. They were loud at Fourth and Fellini, children: their voices rose over the music one of the brothers broadcast from his car stereo—old school "Gin and Juice", Snoop with his mind back on his money, the thump of drum and bass vibrating the street until even the Rausch sisters was shaking their seasoned and privileged booties and the sound-bewildered boy—Aron, Pentheus—backed into traffic.

A cab rushed by, and I confess I flinched, thinking Pentheus was done for, but the cab swerved to miss him and clipped instead a brother on a bicycle, who tumbled to the curb and faked dismemberment and agony until he saw nobody was studying him, so he got up and looked for someone to blame. And that was Aron Starr, of course, or Pentheus, who had crossed Fourth to the southeast corner of the intersection and was perched atop the Church of Christ, with nowhere to run now. I was fixing to call out, to say *go back down the street to rehearsals, son, or better yet I'll take you there since Mr. Thorne needs the chorus.* But then the brother pointed to Aron and started yelling at him. And since the cabbie was rushing past York Street by now, headed downtown, it was hard to blame the brother, who was after all an innocent bystander brushed by swift immutable metal, his accusation the missed shot by the archer that always gets the tragedy going, and it was Aron, or Pentheus, or Aron who got the shaft.

The shouting ignited the crowd. Now the boy climbed the down spout, which buckled to his heaviness, and most of the mob started to cross Fourth toward the scene of approaching accident. One of the god's aunts stood drunkenly south of the intersection and stopped traffic, because of course any *sparagmos*—any sacrificial tearing of flesh—demands a drunk Republican woman as a crossing guard.

By this time Pentheus or Aron had pulled himself up onto what they used to call a parapet, and the accusing brother tried to follow, seeing it had gotten way out of hand, that his initial anger at the boy had unleashed a tide. He tried climbing the spout himself, tried to make peace even at this late hour, but the thin aluminum was giving way under his weight as well, so one of the girls tried it. And she climbed the side of the church like a twining plant, and another followed after her, and soon there were four of them up with Aron and stalking him slowly as he climbed over the arch in search of safety on the other side.

And people under him all the way, shouting for him to jump.

If he'd made it to the back of the church, he would of made it. He could of followed the wide alley into the shadows, have lost his pursuers. From there, Aron could of headed back to the park by roundabout and even returned for rehearsals, become Pentheus in the theatre rather than in the intersection, as though he had never passed through Fourth and Fellini. And he could of gone in protection and cover, because Daddy Chrome and DJ Mel and me were headed to the rescue by now, even when we saw the empty wine bottles being broken on the curb, saw them in the hands of the women above and below, and people tearing the metal of the downspout into bludgeons. The Brischords were headed his way, and the boy would of made it, would of stepped away from this, out of bad drag and into the clean tunic of a prince.

But Maia stepped aloft then, boosted to the cornice by a

gaunt young woman with yellowed eyes. She held out her arms to console or to snatch at the reeling boy. And when Pentheus—when Aron—saw her, he lost his will and most of his balance. He staggered and raised his arms, at first like he was warding things off, but a hot wind passed from west to east, and it slammed me against the store front, and Aron felt it on the parapet, where he stumbled and just gave up.

Or maybe gave in. Because down he fell on the north side of the church, into the crowd, who fell on him like a pack of scavengers, and it all went quiet except for the rending and his lonely scream.

I knew that the snake had been unleashed. I knew it was the breath of the god, not the one in the mask, but the one at the heart of the passion. For the gods appear in many forms, and they carry unwelcome things.

What you think will happen, won't. What you least expect, will. It's the way the gods roll, and I remember it all.

(Exit T. TOMMY BRISCOE. Manent POLYMNIA and THE MUSES, who ascend from the orchestra to the stage).

62. Episode: Anagnorisis

Polymnia: Stephen regrets inviting her already. After all, Muriel swallows attention whole.

That morning the hexagram had roiled with changeable lines, bifurcating to endless and multiple meaning as though the oracle was playing out its last warnings, doubling itself into a silence of too much possibility.

The superior man does not quit the courtyard out his door, but the regulations are severe and difficult, and even with firm corrections there will be evil.

Waters of the abyss over the joyous lake.

The whole production has been a mess of limitations. Even, Stephen thinks, with firm corrections. If there was any other cast member who could disappear on him, Stephen would like to know, and certainly before the curtain goes up. Everyone had switched roles too often for comfort: he worries that the actors will mingle the lines of one character with another's. The music is a recording now, because his hopes for an original score have dissolved with Vincent De Chevre.

If the entire run-up to the play was not entangled and irritating enough, Peter Koenig and wife have shown up. To dress rehearsals instead of opening night. Not only early, but uncomfortably so, both half-reclining on the outdoor tiers in pairs of jeans obviously bought and ironed for the occasion. No theatre crowd would greet them, and Stephen, in a moment's compassion, thinks of sitting beside them, offering amenities and welcome. But he still rankles at the previous encounter, fully suspects that Koenig was not here as a lover of the arts, and factors it all as yet one more fissure in the fickle Tao.

Stephen holds his breath, recalls the stable lines of the hexagram, looks for a rhyming steadiness in the evening.

Thalia: He can trust in George for a workmanlike, if fulsome, performance as the blind prophet Tireisias. Dolores is a pro, despite her erratic behavior of late and her checkered history (and he was part of that checkering, could not blame her so much): she will be here, will smooth Aron's ruffles. Apparently Jack and Apache are reliable as well: he'd received a text on his cell phone from the big, surly gofer stating that *Jack hr np*. He deciphers the encouragement, then turns to anguish over the chorus, knowing that vagrant drunks made for an unreliable work force. But there is T Tommy in the wings, robed and ready, gesticulating over something to another masked figure identifiable by mullet as Daddy Chrome.

So maybe it will work out at last. Maybe this will be the story of one of those productions with a heart, whose rag-tag, loveable crew braves through setbacks to put on a plucky show affirming middle-class American values. Sort of a Judy Garland-Mickey Rooney *Bacchae* for Antioch and the new millennium, he thinks, and shudders.

Melpomene: But of course, that is the stuff of comedy, upon which Sister Thalia smiles vacantly.

And this, as Stephen has almost forgotten, is *The Bacchae*. Where the only ones laughing are the gods.

Thalia: As they sat in the slowly filling amphitheater, Muriel Thorne draws the audience. Friends of Stephen's pay court upon the tiers, and she suns in their attentions. Of course she is the director's mother, she says. She has a right to be critical, so nobody else need comment in media, whether broadcast or print or that vicious little internet.

Muriel glowers at Wade Abner, and for a moment Stephen marvels that his mother is taking his side, until he remembers a young critic's scathing review of her performance in *A Doll's House* back in the sixties, and realizes Muriel's vanity holds a long and well-tied line.

It is too hot outside, she tells him. This park is full of mosquitoes, and why doesn't the city spray the little bloodsuckers into oblivion? That can't bode well, because uncomfortable atmosphere will not make the likes of Wade any more pleasant.

Stephen can count on her support, she confides. No matter the reviews.

With clenched jaw he excuses himself, heading back stage to dress as Cadmus. Billy Shepard trots breathlessly up the sidewalk toward the theatre, laughs and shakes his head apologetically, saying it is a good thing he had come in by Sixth Street, that Fourth is crowded with some ruckus and you know the police, they'll get there when they can.

Stephen ignores this news entirely, bound for the makeshift tiring room where he comes face to face with the hysterical George Castille.

"Oh sweet dramatic Jesus," the old actor stage-whispers, his wide eye-liner simulating some kind of school-play blindness as he waves and gestures toward the audience. "Two of your principals are late."

It is like the world dropping away. Stephen steadies himself against a tree, stares off into desolation. "God damn it, George," he mutters. "What do we do?"

"It should be fine, Mr. Thorne," assures a voice behind him, reedy and melodious. He does not recognize it as Jack until he turns and sees the boy smiling in front of him, clad in a purple tunic gashed with dark copper red.

"Really, Mr. Thorne. Swear to God. Aron went to get his mom a few minutes ago. They're scarcely two blocks away by now, I'm certain."

Melpomene: Stephen looks south toward the Court and Hill Street beyond it, his thoughts not allowing that the two would be coming from the disrupted north, where Billy claimed some kind of riot is simmering. He strains his eyes toward two forms approaching in the summer dusk, hugging the brick wall that cornered Fourth and Magnolia.

He believes, he wants to believe, that it is Aron and Dolores, so he takes Jack by the arm, perhaps even roughly, and points toward the shadowy, still-distant figures.

"Your eyes are younger, Jack," he says, the statement more question and plea.

Jack nods. "Sure looks like them, don't it?"

In desperation, Stephen murmurs agreement, hoping that things would settle and right themselves and even the changing lines fall into solidity and balance. Surely the worst has happened.

He looks up as the music started, astounded that Jack had cued Apache Downs and the tape is rolling, the first lurching bars of Led Zeppelin's "Kashmir," that brew of exoticism, ecstasy and narcosis. Jack is off to the stage, heedless of Stephen's direction. Stephen calls aloud to stop, to wait, but the dress rehearsal is in motion, T. Tommy leading the robed Brischords to their orchestra space in front of the stage where they stand and wait, swaying to the music.

63. Episode: Out of the Machine

(Exeunt MUSES, only MELPOMENE remaining).

Melpomene: The god descends on Jack, and the air unravels.

He moves downstage and stands at the apron, the expectant eyes of his derelict chorus turned upward, as though in admiration. He grows in the lights, his shadow lengthening, thickening, gathering substance as Apache brings down the music and the crowd falls hush.

Even Muriel is quiet, surrendered to the god's incarnation as Jack begins to speak, standing contrapposto like a classical statue, the thyrsis in his hand bristling with borrowed light:

> *I am Dionysos, come here to Thebes,*
> *I am the son of Zeus, delivered in fire*
> *from Semele, the daughter of Cadmus,*
> *my father's lightning the midwife.*
> *Now have I changed form, taken human shape*

> *to present myself at the springs of Dirce*
> *at the waters of Ismenus.*

He holds the wand aloft, and in the trees surrounding the sequestered amphitheater, the birds settle in the branches, among them my sisters transfigured, their duties over, their time to watch begun. It is ecstatic, sexual, the way the thyrsus in the boy's hand—cardboard tubing wrapped half-heartedly by Apache Downs with green pipe-cleaner—suddenly flourishes with vines, with grapes that empurpurated swiftly in the bent light.

I am beside myself. I moan, hoping nobody hears, that the dream stays unbroken.

(Exit MELPOMENE. She continues to speak from off stage).

Jack is the first of the antipodes, the first spark of ignition. I yearn for him or for the god his occupant, as I meld with the night and vanish, but my sisters know where I am headed, and I know the next step in the story.

For a moment there is unstable, sacral space. And then the drum pounds from a distance to signal the chaos approaching.

Down Fourth the women come from the intersection, glowing corposants, dancing in jubilant disarray, stumbling, calling out, their cries rushing up to their throats from deep in their loins, their arms and clothing torn as though they have passed through briars to emerge here on a city sidewalk, stunned by the passage. At the head of the crowd walks Dolores, her mouth and chin bloodied as though she has been struck, placing one foot before the other with a kind of staggering gravity, like a drunken driver asked to walk the imaginary line. Supported by a Rausch sister at each arm, she holds aloft a bundle, a weight in a sack, all three women regally, formally posed like the fountain statuary to their south, a stable, gliding tableau in the midst of the whirling arms and legs of the crack-heads, whores, transvestites and beggars who have accompanied them from the intersection.

Peter Koenig stands up in the crowd, shields his eyes and gazes out toward the approaching procession. He understands the nature of sacrifice, and if anyone sees where this is headed it is the high priest of Antioch, his Maraleese tugging at his belt uncomprehendingly, as now Dolores Starr steps into the theatre light and the air swims and buckles.

You can smell the wine and blood. You can hear drunken Elvis at the head of the chorus…

> *O Thebes, nurse of Semele! crown yourself with ivy;*
> *blossom with bindweed, and join the procession*
> *with boughs of oak and pine*
> *the whole land is dancing, when the god*
> *leads his revelers to the hills, where maidens await,*
> *roused from loom and shuttle…*

their chant lost now in the outcry when the procession moves through the audience, and the spectators notice the blood that gloves the hands of the women, that paints their lips and cheeks and the bottom of the sack Dolores carries.

Stephen and George step forward now, the play past their grasp, action and word riding the hot current of the god's will and the mounting will of those present. Nobody wants to want this, but everyone knows in their deepest heart that they have wished it from the moment they could wish, that the current they heard pulsing and driving in the wombs of their mothers has brought them to this night, this moment, the sodden bag held aloft in Dolores' slick red hands.

> *Oh! happy that celebrant who falls to earth*
> *out of the riot in his holy fawnskin robe,*
> *chasing the goat to drink its blood,*
> *sweet raw flesh as he hurries to Phrygia*
> *or to Libya's hills, ahead of him the god*
> *exults with cries of Evoe! Evoe!*

Dolores Starr shouts above the tumult how good she had been, how dutiful, how all the men who stand in wing and waiting should be proud, how she gave the lion the first blow.

She opens the dripping bag, and something falls to the gravel beside Peter and Maraleese Koenig. Maraleese cries out, and the Reverend lurched to his feet, dragging his wife out of the wake of the unspeakable. Dolores staggers toward the stage and turned the bag inside out. And there in the orchestra, where once the chorus danced the dithyramb to the arriving god, she empties the rest of its contents into the orchestra.

And the wet sound of her son's head falling is all that is heard in the world.

64. Exodos: Strophe: T. Tommy and Polymnia

Tommy: The police record on the matter is sketchy, children. You would think that cable news would drip all bloody and commentators would feast on the remains of poor Pentheus. But the story slides toward silence, its details like the faintest crust of pigment or wine or blood on carved figures.

I heard the paranoia pick it up on the second day. Apache Downs' weekly blog told a story that all ten readers dismissed as science-fictional reverie, as something Lovecraft and eldritch and not even Apache's best work. A huge python lurked and did not lurk, he said, in the recesses of a theatre, where it swallowed and did not swallow cast and audience of a play's dress rehearsal. He set forth rumor, then speculation undercutting rumor until "Has Anybody Seen Jack Rausch?" remained a question unanswerable, one that went internet viral and keeps on spreading.

But there might of been others.

Polymnia: Apache claimed twenty people missing, though by the time he posted, all but four had surfaced, some of them talking about the horrific disruption of the play, how it broke the frame with vengeance until they thought the procession was real. By now they had heard the story, the actress going crazy in the role like a suicide Judas at Oberammergau. But though the jury was out on the deeds and whereabouts of Dolores Starr, Apache Downs' snake turned into a metaphor in the blogosphere, even the most conspiracy-minded of the floating trolls out there calling it metaspeculation, a symbol of how local authority, government in general, the capitalist machinery or the Obama Administration had "swallowed the evidence and the offenders." It was Vince Foster floating in the Potomac once more, 9/11 as an inside job or the fifty-year deep six of a birth certificate.

Tommy: And whatever myth they brung to the dance was the myth they kept on believing.

The police worked hard, but slow as usual. They had trouble finding witnesses after the tumult, for Falcon and Chrome and Mel and I lost ourselves in the shelters to await our Reunion and Vegas Commemorative , headed to a park in your neighborhood on the sixteenth of August when the signs go up on the overpasses. Eventually I seen it as my civic duty, and told the Brischords to lie low, that I would take on the tricky country of public relations.

So when the police asked, I described myself as resident at large, told them how the snake story was literally true fact, brothers and sisters. That after Agave's unveiling, or Dolores's, the audience had scattered. Not that they were many to begin with, no more than a dozen at a dress rehearsal. Some were scared, some disgusted, Wade Abner thought it was performance art but not very edgy. When they all left the theater it was like this huge wave of malice had passed over us all, and the girls from Fourth and Fellini slunk back into the dark, since they figured the show must be over and they weren't getting paid none.

The aunts of the god and young Maia, they wandered off into the park. I heared the congressman took them all in, the little blonde girl included. That he has soothed her parents with the promise to take care of the little maenad. That his sisters stand testimony to his history of providing.

Only the reverend and his wife remained, and some old woman fear-struck or simply old, I could not be sure, but she wasn't or couldn't move. The wind began to rise, overturning stage props and wrenching free the rafters of the theatre. Then I swear, and this I told the police, that the old woman began to change, to transmogrify in the crazy moon, the shadow of the trees passing over her like it was molding her into a new shape. And there she was, the python Apache wrote about. She turned and coiled, slithering down the tiers toward the orchestra, where my entourage and I stood fascinated, because the legends is true when it come to the hypnosis of serpents.

It was the boss coming on stage that deflected her attention. Mr. Thorne come downstage with Mr. Castille, and the python wrapped around him and unhinged her jaw, and I was just too horrified to think I had been gonna step up about a hundred dollars more to show on opening night, suddenly that seemed like backseat driving when you put it up against what was taking down Mr. Thorne, because the snake curled around him and began to crush, and we were out of there and Mr. Castille, who at least had more cojones than MelMel or Chrome in that he struck once the serpent, he bruised her head with his heel before he, too, high-tailed it into the night and denial.

Then the python unhinged her jaw, and the unspeakable began.

We got ourselves saved again later on, at Antioch that October. Because them things need renewal as well, and we heard there was coffee and sandwiches.

They was no hippie bus this time to get us there, but Miss Maia give us bus fare. That time of day on a Sunday there is no express out that way, but we traveled on transfers, and I have learned that there is no place far from you when you do.

We knew, when we got to the complex, that we were not the kind of sinners that the Reverend Koenig wanted to save. Our sins were warm ones, borne of too much wine and naughty loving, and these days they welcomed the cooler sinners there, the frauds and inside traders. They had ways of explaining how these were not sins, not really, but ours remained most grievous, most cardinal.

They claimed nothing had changed. But Koenig had changed. Had become more like them, had rejoined the fold. I had not thought he would give in, for I had heard things about him. But that night he stepped down from the pulpit and stalked the stage, like an actor or like a big wild cat. He was enthusiastic, and I suppose the god had picked him out of the multitude, had found him useful for the time.

Because it all changes, children. I have no idea how many times I have been saved: I remember wearing a leisure suit once, when I opened my heart to Jesus. I remember a field far earlier, high grass and women singing, when I was a boy in the country. I believe there might of been once when they did not call it saving and when they spoke in a tongue I no longer recall. Each time the god descends he expects tribute, he expects blood and ashes. And maybe the Reverend Koenig was figuring that out, or maybe just riding the snake until the loneliness made sense and he could rest in it.

I do know that Miss Maia has receded, like the Rausch sisters, into obscurity and money, and that the Congressman's women have taken her in, are guiding her, making her respectable and putting the tags on things. She may even marry, but I think it is too soon to tell, what with her work and the election weeks away.

She is the one who visits Miss Starr when the schedule permits. The whole revelation, the blood and the police and the anagnorisis, all took place in the hospital wings. They keep her lulled there pending slow therapy, settled on an anti-psychotic cocktail that makes a man downright envious. Miss Starr is thinner now, almost gaunt, and that if she stands by the windows of the ward the light shines through her, and you can see the bars and the glass and the muted promise of sun beyond it.

I am fading as well now. I noticed it when we first broke into fall weather, back a couple of weeks ago, when I awakened on the park bench again, covered with cold dew. There was a dream I was rising from, somewhere in a warm night so clear and star-struck that it was hardly night. I did not recognize the constellations, or perhaps we had yet to name them and give them meaning. But in the dream I was rushing through undergrowth, not away from anything or toward anything, not really, but with the joy of running, children. It felt like that moment when I copy the King, and mimic his movement, the pivot of leg and knee, the roll of the scarf behind his neck, the martial karate dance that he done in Vegas.

It was that moment when you are not yourself but flowing, on a current you remember only when you enter it, bound toward that deep and common destination, and for that moment you are so in tune with it all, joy and tears, that when the dream fades and you find yourself on the bench covered with October dew and the sunlight bare and bald above the rows of shrubbery and trees, there's a great sadness that takes you, and you cry to dream that vital peace once more.

(Exit TOMMY. Manet POLYMNIA, who moves upstage toward a lowering backdrop that shows a procession of MUSES in black-figure silhouette)

Polymnia: The sarcophagus as refuge, as consoling stillness.

We take a different marching order now. To trick beholders with our processional. Already the girls exchange lutes, scrolls, podia. We cover our tracks, and the generations to come will know each sister by the name of another.

Across from us the krater settles into stillness as well. The god and his Ariadne, the maenads and the glittering *pappasilenos*, the contending boys on the opposite side—all of them would look familiar right now, if you have been following the story and know the principal actors. But right now, it is after hours: nobody here but the scarcely animate statuary, the god of fluorescent light, the wanton security guard.

And the peopled krater, of course, breathing with the memory of wine.

The countenance of the god is young, then older, then back to young. As always in portrayal—young, feminine and beautiful, then bearded and wiry like the satyric goats he musters. This time he darkens, his skin softening and his eyes folding in a serene and indifferent loveliness, and then the painted profile takes on skin more pale, stippled shadow at the jaw, the shorter, swept-back hair recognizable from the pulpit of Antioch, from pulpits all across America, for that matter. The woman opposite him plays the twinned reeds of the *aulos*, but she is young and old as well—an Ariadne bridal at last, or a mother drawn out into the Dionysian forest on a current of wine and madness. And the old man changes the least, grey-haired paunchiness with occasional sideburns and a costume glitter to his robe.

And that old man carries a krater as well, upon it another old *silenos* carrying a krater, receding into the depths of the mysteries. He just told you he was fading. I look upon him— upon them all—and thank my mother Memory, who has given me the final word.

The krater is brimful with imagined wine. You can drink from it, of course. No blame. The gods say so, as do the hexagrams. But if you wet your head, my dears, you lose everything.

The time is coming for sleep again. The banners outside the museum are dated, and the crate readied that will take us across your huge and dormant country to another venue. I would say we shall wake again and you will see us, but *night is perpetual sleep*, as the poet says. So I will not know until it happens. Until then I will come to the banks of the dark underground river and wait there, and the krater will settle into sleep as well, the gods translated and fallow in impossible light.

About the Author

Over the past 25 years, Michael Williams has written a number of strange novels, from the early Weasel's Luck and Galen Beknighted in the best-selling DRAGONLANCE series to the more recent lyrical and experimental Arcady, singled out for praise by Locus and Asimov's magazines. In Trajan's Arch, his eleventh novel, stories fold into stories and a boy grows up with ghostly mentors, and the recently published Vine mingles Greek tragedy and urban legend, as a local dramatic production in a small city goes humorously, then horrifically, awry.

Trajan's Arch and Vine are two of the books in Williams's highly anticipated City Quartet, to be joined in 2018 by Dominic's Ghosts and Tattered Men.

Williams was born in Louisville, Kentucky, and spent much of his childhood in the south central part of the state, the red-dirt gothic home of Appalachian foothills and stories of Confederate guerrillas. Through good luck and a roundabout journey he made his way through through New England, New York, Wisconsin, Britain and Ireland, and has ended up less than thirty miles from where he began. He has a Ph.D. in Humanities, and teaches at the University of Louisville, where he focuses on the he Modern Fantastic in fiction and film. He is married, and has two grown sons.